ARE YOU REALLY HAPPY?

Fundamental Happiness

~ Deepak Chatterjee ~

EMBASSY BOOKS
www.embassybooks.in

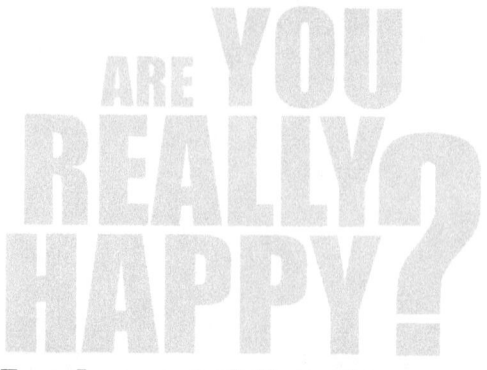

Fundamental Happiness

Copyright © 2013 by Deepak Chatterjee

First published in India 2013

Published in India by :

EMBASSY BOOK DISTRIBUTORS
120, Great Western Building,
Maharashtra Chamber of Commerce Lane,
Kala Ghoda, Fort,
Mumbai- 400 023.

Tel : (+91-22) 22819546 / 32967415
Email : info@embassybooks.in

ISBN : 978-93-81860-92-2

Acknowledgements

I consider myself extraordinarily fortunate to have questioned life and existence early in life. I spent many years in distress and despair, until I discovered the FUNDAMENTAL HAPPINESS that resides within all of us, but eludes us. I am grateful to Nature for having given me the sensitivity necessary to feel myself completely and fully, for having given me the authenticity to accept and acknowledge myself and for having given me the courage to face the ugliness within, to be able to transcend it and find joy.

I am grateful to one of my psychiatrists, Dr. Chandan Gupta, for being patient with me and discussing with me dimensions of life beyond the usual objective and clinical treatment. Two eminent philosophers, US based existential writer James Leonard Park and Canada based Eckhart Tolle completely changed my life. I am hugely indebted to them. I discovered more such writers and was happy to note that non-religious spirituality was evolving as a very useful area of interest in an increasingly troubled world. I found it to be fully amenable to science and modern thought.

My employer for 35 years, State Bank of India, took me many places within India and abroad. I place on record my gratitude to this great institution for giving me the opportunity of extraordinary experiences far beyond banking – of life and people. I also got a stint as a Behavioural Science Faculty at State Bank

Academy, Gurgaon. There I first had to be trained by a senior, Achla Sethi. I owe to her the courage and authenticity to take the very first truthful peek at myself. Throughout my journey towards FUNDAMENTAL HAPPINESS, I had one steady companion by my side, my wife Chandra. She has been my sounding board for all my dilemmas in life. My daughters, Madurima and Arunima helped me remember how the human tentativeness is part of very young lives too and how it manifests in sensitive persons as they grow up. Together, as a family, we always question each other and interact on this sensitive subject. The quality of such discussions has been of great help to me while shaping my thoughts for this book.

I also express my gratitude to my colleagues Srinivas Jain and Sakshi Dalela who helped me with ideas on social media and publicity.

I am grateful to Sohin Lakhani, CEO of Embassy Books, my publisher, for resonating with my thoughts, to Puja Kashyap for editorial support and to Anchal Agarwal Bansal for coming out with interesting sketches for the book.

Foreword by Dr. Chandan Gupta, Psychiatrist

In one of Francis Bacon's essays *Of Truth*, he wrote, "'*What is truth*?' said jesting Pilate, and would not stay for an answer". In attempting to comment on what is happiness or for that matter "Fundamental Happiness", I am tempted to follow suit. However, to be happy is a universal angst. Did happiness start from the most primitive of organisms, unicellular bacteria and now has reached a billion dollar effort to promote and provide happiness for the human race? Rabindranath Tagore in a short poem, talks of the joy of a "Spark", which illuminates for a millionth of a second and disappears, paving the way for us to sense happiness in "being".

Children are undoubtedly happy when they have the freedom to be on their own. They laugh, giggle, run around for no rhyme or reason which adults find inane and irksome. They are adept at creating their own world of genuine happiness with or without toys. Thus, we humans are obviously endowed with an impulsive quality of being joyful. In Bengal the institution of "*addaa*" symbolises a camaraderie, a happiness without strings over endless cups of tea.

The founders of the American Constitution recognised this ephemeral quality of happiness in human beings, and in their wisdom, or was it haste, incorporated in their Declaration of Independence "the pursuit of happiness" as a fundamental right; as though if not so enshrined, happiness would play truant and escape from the inhabitant's psyche, taking a leisurely stroll around the earth while retaining its freedom, popping up and touching peoples' lives spontaneously elsewhere. Is happiness a quarry to be pursued and captured? Can happiness ever mean a duty bound obligatory activity? The philosophers of yore have waxed eloquently in defining and redefining this endearing attribute in living creatures specially human beings. I must hasten to add that the quest for happiness predates the Declaration of Independence. Lord Krishna said "Do your duty, do not look for the fruits thereof". He was prudent not to define the fruits he was referring to. Were they material gains which, if they did not materialise, would render us unhappy or was it something abstract not linked to anything in the material sense, thus giving us the option to be happy on our own terms and not dependent on the whims and fancies of the world around us?

The seeking of happiness is a complicated process. All of us are involved in it at a personal cum family level or in the larger context involving society. Being a social creature, our happiness is inevitably entwined with the happiness of the emotional world of others around us. So a governmental factor also enters the picture.

In that sense the American Declaration of Independence regarding the pursuit of happiness echoes Adam Smith's statement: "The happiness of society is the end of Government." Yet, the world over, society is riddled with Librium and Prozac, and chemically mediated "happiness" seems to be the order of the day and spreading like bush fire. Thus Deepak Chatterjee's "Fundamental Happiness" takes on a special relevance in creating an awareness wherein lies our happiness.

Writing a Foreword must be an onerous task particularly for someone who can hardly claim to be a man of letters. This becomes even more daunting when the subject of the book probes the recesses of the mind for answers seeking fundamental happiness. I met Deepak Chatterjee more than two decades ago. Fundamentally, I attempted to change the co-ordinates of his perception about life and minimise the morbidity of the thought processes that engulfed him. It is deeply gratifying to see him embarking upon a self-exploratory journey, which through the generations have been explored by many a great mind in their own unique ways, lighting up lamps of enlightenment for us to traverse, if we choose to do so. The author is one of those who have opted to walk along these paths, sharing with us their experiences. It is the human race's curiosity and endeavor to find answers in so many diverse realms of our existence, the physical, the mental and spiritual universes, hoping ultimately to create a unified meaningful matrix, which is as daunting as anything we can imagine.

Experimental psychology has opened many more doors of our brain functions, our cognitive profiles as well as the unique qualities of the plasticity of the brain , revealing the immense capacity to heal itself in different ways, but at the end of the day a healthy brain does not reflect a healthy mind.

The building blocks of life have perhaps revealed more than just the creation of life. Charles Darwin's celebrated book *On the Origin of Species* and his Theory of Evolution opened scientific doors to delve deep within ourselves. Simultaneously we have the benefit of great spiritual masters who in their own way have pushed further the frontiers of this human saga. But the human mind continues to baffle us in a manner which precludes the creation of a map that would neatly help us to move in our own back yards without stumbling; both streams have tried to bring some coherence, understanding and balance in the playing fields of our minds, informing all our strivings with a sense of tranquillity, leading us hopefully to the shores of "Fundamental Happiness".

In this context Deepak Chatterjee's efforts are laudable. His lifelong engagement and sincere efforts in resolving fundamental issues concerning our existence and overall wellbeing have been presented in a lucid, forthright and well-structured manner, thus generating a thought provoking sensitive account in a highly engrossing manner which will keep the readers riveted to this fascinating journey of the mind.

His own experiences along with his extensive readings bear upon his conclusions and will enlighten his readers, cutting across age barriers to look afresh with greater clarity concerning many age old beliefs and teachings, which we have inherited and much too often ignored at our peril.

A very persuasive and powerful manifestation of the mind and its meanderings.

Indeed, it is a great read and one will be tempted to come back to it many a time.

New Delhi,

2013.

Contents

ARE YOU REALLY HAPPY?

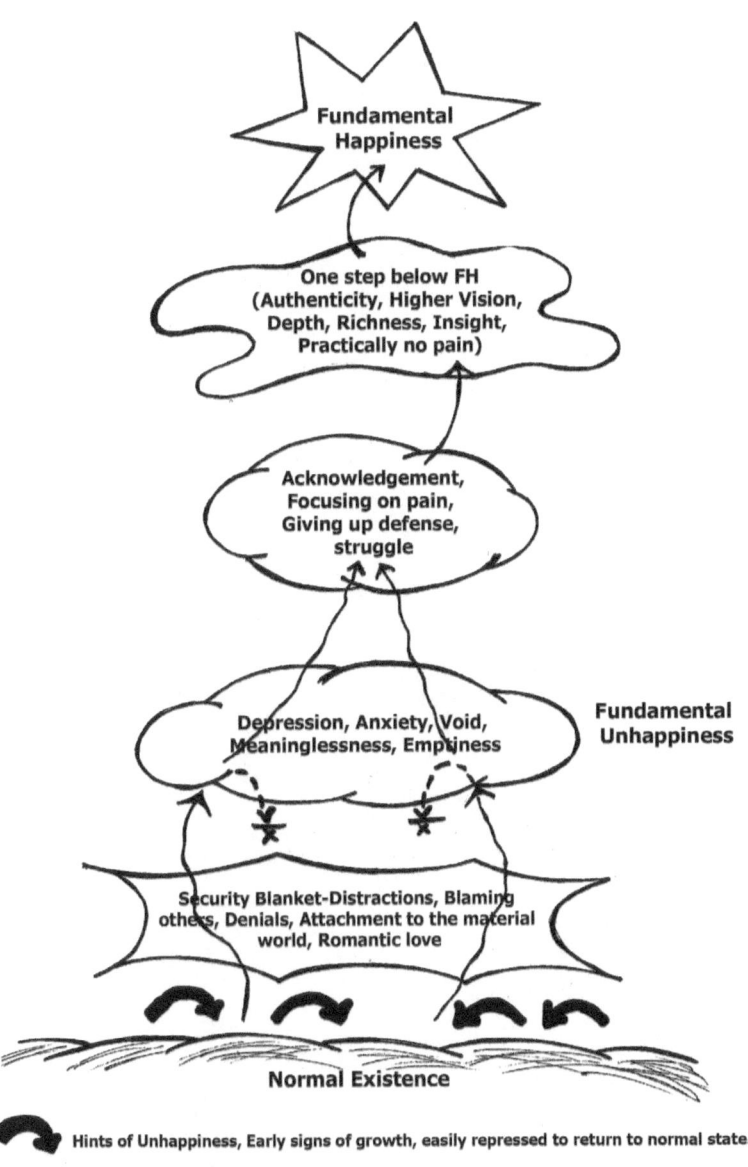

Fundamental
Happiness

One step below FH
(Authenticity, Higher Vision,
Depth, Richness, Insight,
Practically no pain)

Acknowledgement,
Focusing on pain,
Giving up defense,
struggle

Depression, Anxiety, Void,
Meaninglessness, Emptiness

**Fundamental
Unhappiness**

Security Blanket-Distractions, Blaming
others, Denials, Attachment to the material
world, Romantic love

Normal Existence

Hints of Unhappiness, Early signs of growth, easily repressed to return to normal state.

Evolutionary growth witnessed by sensitive people. Experiencing unhappiness or moving beyond

Failed, desperate attempts by unhappy people, through diversions, treatment to return to 'Normal State'. Blocked at 'X'. cannot go back to "Normal"

WHERE ARE YOU?

Have you been suffering from depression or anxiety for no apparent cause?

Do you find life meaningless and full of despair?

Have you been asking fundamental questions about life with no convincing answers?

Do you find yourself running after seemingly important activities, pursuits, while deep within, you sense that you are actually running away from some unknown fear?

Do you feel something is actually missing amidst an otherwise *satisfactory* existence?

Are you afraid of loneliness?

Do you keep your daily life packed with either work or fun, afraid that a blank slot would get you feeling *bored*?

Do you find yourself tensed up and mostly on the short fuse?

Are you the *happy* kind leading a busy and *contended* life, with sometimes a hint at the background of a faint unease or dissatisfaction for no apparent reason?

Is it only a mere suggestion in the backdrop that you are able to

ignore or push away and continue with your busy life?
Does the fear of death haunt you?

This book might give you the answers to many such questions which have been nagging you and may eventually make you feel that FUNDAMENTAL HAPPINESS that resides within all of us, but eludes us. Once you reach there you do not need external props to hold up your happy self, though you can continue to enjoy the usual joys of life. This work is based on my own similar experiences. It also includes comments from psychiatrist, Dr. Chandan Gupta, who was treating me several years ago and gave me some early insights which, coupled with my own experiences, readings and experiments, gave me a life of peace and joy. Depression, despair and melancholy have disappeared from my life. You will also see that if you are indeed living a painful life of uncaused depression, despair, anxiety or meaninglessness, you are actually closer to the FUNDAMENTAL HAPPINESS than most *normal* people are.

WHERE YOU CAN BE...

begin by giving you a brief peek into my own life. I do this to give you a sense of where I was and where I eventually reached. Way back in 1972, I had seen a man lying dead on a street in Delhi, knocked down by a bus. His bicycle lay beside him, with his lunch box still clamped on the rear seat. I naturally felt sad. Everything else continued as before. The morning traffic was at its peak. This event made no difference to the world. The world continued, unchanged. But this man had ceased to exist in the world. I was on my way to college, and I kept thinking about this dead person. He was not known to me, and I kept putting myself in his position. I could also have died like that. I felt how lucky I was to still be alive. Then suddenly a thought came to me: so what that I escaped death this time? Death is inevitable and will come sooner or later. I became numb. The next thought was: how will it be post death? Where will my consciousness go? I just could not accept my impending non-existence. It was as if I had realised this eventual and inevitable non-existence that day for the first time.

When I reached college, I tried asking friends if their impending death upset them in any way. Surprised at my absurd question, their replies were the usual stuff: *'Everyone has to die', 'what is the big deal?'* etc. I could not fathom the casualness with which they were treating their certain death. I was depressed, fearful and tense the whole day. I returned home but did not share anything with my parents. I went to sleep with difficulty, hoping that next morning everything will be fine. But I woke up the next morning with the same despair, depression and anxiety. It was no longer only the fear of death that was haunting me. I began to question everything. What is the basic purpose of life? What are all of us running after? It seemed that my world had changed forever. Also, I could sense that the *down in the dumps* feeling had no longer any connection to the death that I had seen in front of my eyes. That could have been a trigger, but what I was now feeling was more at a fundamental level. I was fundamentally unhappy. From here started a long painful journey of depression, despair, meaninglessness, anxiety lasting several years. Externally I was as *normal* as anyone else. But inside me there was a tornado going on. I tried my best, often successfully, to keep myself involved in pleasant things, having fun with friends, this and that. But my basic questions were stalking me like a dark cloud, at times receding into the background, and often, especially when I was with myself, taking a stranglehold of my being. I thought I had gone mad. Also, I had a lurking sense that this *new* experience was not really new; that I had probably sensed these dilemmas even before, as a child, but that they had been successfully diverted.

I wondered how people around me seemed to be generally happy or content. I started to think that if I had nothing in particular to be happy or satisfied about, it only meant that I would naturally be depressed or anxious. In other words, I asked myself, whether there should always be something out there in the world to keep me happy or satisfied. What, then, is the fundamental level of existence of a human being on a happiness-sadness scale? Young as I was, I tested myself by asking whether things will change if I suddenly became very rich, say by winning a lottery. Or, say some very happy situation was to develop surrounding me. But deep inside the honest answer was bothering me that such events would not make any fundamental difference to the meaninglessness I was sensing. I realised that there was nothing in the external world that could address this FUNDAMENTAL UNHAPPINESS within me. The insistent question that now continuously nagged me was how people around me seemed to be generally happy.

> **THE BIGGEST REVELATION WAS THAT THE UNCAUSED DEPRESSION THAT I WAS SUFFERING FROM WAS NOT A MENTAL DISEASE. IT WAS, IN FACT, A SIGN OF GROWTH! I MADE A PARADIGM INTERNAL SHIFT IN LIFE SOMETIME LATER, AND SOON I WAS A CHANGED PERSON.**

I did my rounds with psychiatrists. I broadly encountered two kinds. Most would hear me out, come to the conclusion that I was suffering from depression and then medicate me. A few would engage in long discussions. One of them, Dr. Chandan Gupta, not only spent a long time on each session, he actually engaged with me in all the questions that I had encountered. He did not dismiss the fundamental questions about life that I had to ask. He also did medicate me, but I found him to be more than a psychiatrist – a philosopher, who too was touched by basic questions of life. It was always a pleasure to talk to him. In one of my discussions with him on seeking meaning in life, he mentioned existentialism.

Having got the lead on existentialism, I read a number of books and searched the internet on the subject. Years later I stumbled upon the writings of two individuals who changed my life forever. The first individual is James Leonard Park, a US based existential philosopher whose major book, *Our Existential Predicament:*

Loneliness, Depression, Anxiety & Death, is available on the internet in parts. The full book has to be ordered directly from him. The second individual is Eckhart Tolle, a Canada based spiritual writer, whose books *The Power of Now* and *A New Earth* had a profound impact on me. The biggest revelation was that the uncaused depression that I was suffering from was not a mental disease. It was, in fact, a sign of growth! I made a paradigm internal shift in life sometime later, and soon I was a changed person.

The rest of this book is about the details and the nature of this shift. Depression left me in a matter of months. And, I never needed any medication or psychiatric help for depression or anxiety. I have, since then, tasted the FUNDAMENTAL HAPPINESS humans are endowed with, and I am able to witness the external world from a better vantage. In general, I am a more cheerful being, and do not look for external support for sustaining my happiness. However, that does not prevent me from enjoying things in life. Rather, I am in a position to enjoy them even more for I do not cling to them since I have no fear of losing them.

This book will give you the insights into how this is possible. I can state it upfront, though you will find more details about the process and the steps as you read this book, the way out of this basic suffering is through it, and not away from it. In other words, instead of diverting away from this fundamental pain, the solution lies in embracing the pain, accepting it, witnessing it, without analysing it, and then finding the FUNDAMENTAL HAPPINESS which too is firmly embedded within us. I say this based on my own experience. Interestingly my external life did not change at all.

I was working in the financial sector and I continue to do so – in a fairly senior position now – a CEO. Most of my daily acquaintances are not aware of the changes inside me. Externally I remain the same. Some of the more perceptive kind did notice that I appear very peaceful and tranquil, yet, also confident. I have had one co-passenger in my entire journey: my wife. She knew about my sufferings all through, and also was by my side during my remission. Being a teacher of Literature, she had had her own exposure to a lot of philosophical writings, and already knew many things that I learnt later. She empathized but never lectured me. That was good because these sensitive aspects are best understood through your own experience rather than a lecture session.

A word of caution: Some of you could be speculating that you are in for a heavy dose of philosophy. I promise that there will be none of that. Some would wonder whether I am going to lecture on existentialism. Again, while I do respect that school of thought, I am not trapped there, and you are going to have none of the grim writings on existentialism. I believe that existentialism is a must-be-there stepping stone. One must go beyond that. Finally, I have not leaned on any religious beliefs. In fact you do not need any religious affiliation for release from the basic human suffering. Also, your current religious affiliation will not be questioned by anything that I have written hereafter. Neither am I going to recommend that you move to seclusion and start living like a hermit. You will mostly find simple interesting examples from your daily experiences, which offer us valuable insights, but we mostly tend to miss them. The FUNDAMENTAL HAPPINESS deep inside us belongs to us, and we can have it for free. Once you are fundamentally happy, you do not crave for external props to maintain your happiness. Yet you keep enjoying the external world without becoming addicted to it. You can still go to a pub and enjoy your beer. It just needs some basic understanding and awareness; and, a lot of commitment. So, read on.

3

FUNDAMENTAL
UNHAPPINESS

How many of us can sense or agree that we are fundamentally unhappy beings?

Even those who consider themselves very happy would admit at times, to a creeping sense of dissatisfaction within.

One does not have to be a pessimist to sense that.

With a certain degree of inner sensitivity, one can sense it.

If you have the courage and honesty to accept that, you have taken the first big step towards a new life. You can be a hardcore optimist, look at the brighter side of things and still discover the basic unease.

You are only being truthful and authentic.

Those who agree that there is general dissatisfaction within might quickly list what is wrong with their circumstances. For them the cause of the dissatisfaction is *external*.

The basic human condition and the FUNDAMENTAL UNHAPPINESS embedded in it are missed out.

Sensitive and insightful persons are not able to fool themselves about their circumstances, and could get into uncaused depression and run to a psychiatrist. They could lead wretched lives filled with depression, anxiety and despair. Psychiatrists are almost certain to treat them for clinical depression through medication. That such depression and unease could be a manifestation of the fundamental human condition at the level of spirit, and not mind or body, is yet to be fully appreciated by the psychiatric community.

I have myself struggled with similar suffering, and have felt the uncaused depression, anxiety and despair. I understand the dilemma that many of you face in a similar predicament. That dilemma arises from the interaction between two kinds of dissatisfaction – that from within and from without. Because they mix up, we are not able to recognize the more basic form of dissatisfaction.

Actually the two kinds of dissatisfaction feed off each other as illustrated in the following diagram.

Existencial Dissatisfaction

Circumstancial Dissatisfaction

Dissatisfaction could arise because of our internal or external conditions. We often blame it only on the external. While circumstantial dissatisfaction often triggers the existential unease deep within us, whatever existential dissatisfaction we may feel is confused with and blamed on the circumstances.

It is a two way process.

The trick lies in identifying and focusing on our basic underlying condition.

As you read on, you will see that the way out of suffering is to fully face and acknowledge all the pain, no matter whether circumstantial or fundamental. Do not get too much into whether what you are suffering is due to an external cause or it is arising from within, for you will quickly lapse into a mental exercise. Whereas, if you focus only on the pain and deeply feel it without probing it you will learn how to truthfully observe yourself.

Accept that we human beings have a core, which is fundamentally unhappy.

Beneath that is yet another core that is fundamentally happy.

It helps just to know this.

Let's take a look at ourselves without our support systems and props we are so attached to.

Our strong love for these things makes them an extension of us.

We get defined by our belongings, riches, successes, and attachments.

So we have no chance of feeling ourselves at the fundamental level.

Humanity has tried to come to terms with this basic human tentativeness for thousands of years. Mankind was scared and did not know how to deal with it. Mythology helped to partly *explain* and partly distract. Most religions of the world were born out of the fact that they had to address this suffering to help humanity move beyond. For most of us, following religious texts has not been easy. I have devoted a separate section on religion subsequently in this book. Some wise and courageous men and women realized the need for working at the level of spirit. But most of them got entangled with religion or were slotted as holy men or women by their followers. Hence no solution reached the suffering masses. Fortunately, we now have the benefit of the shared experiences and writings of many learned persons, which can be beneficial to us. Internet and social media have helped tremendously. Yet, there is still a fair degree of myth surrounding such knowledge. The entire subject matter needs to be de-mystified.

Many wise persons gave up their practical lives and lived in isolation to feel their basic existence and then to experience that fundamental joy within.

They became enlightened beings.

As I promised you in the beginning, I am not suggesting a similar course of action.

I have myself not done that.

All I want to say is that internally sensitive persons have been able to notice their underlying unease.

Importantly also, please recognize that plain uncaused depression or a sense of meaninglessness and emptiness is not a mental disease.

On the contrary, if you are going through that, you could be ready to move higher and taste a different life of FUNDAMENTAL HAPPINESS.

Such unease is then, a sign of spiritual growth.

Most of you would have heard or read about Victor Frankl. He was an Austrian neurologist and psychiatrist as well as a Holocaust survivor. Based on his experience in concentration camps, he developed his model of existential therapy and became a prominent source of inspiration for humanistic psychologists. He has written in his book *The Will to Meaning*, *"there is no need to feel ashamed of existential despair because of the assumption that it is an emotional disease, for it is not a neurotic symptom but a human achievement and accomplishment. Above all it is a manifestation of intellectual sincerity and honesty"* (Quoted by James Park). Today we have many such authentic people who have moved beyond and are living joyful lives. It is my intention to come out, through this book, with a step-by-step approach to fully and honestly acknowledging ourselves and then moving on to a life closer to FUNDAMENTAL HAPPINESS.

If you have doubts about the reality of this very tentative and fundamentally unhappy nature of human beings, there are numerous examples of excellent plays, movies, books and paintings that have captured the basic unease of human existence. That hollowness or emptiness within has been brilliantly captured in the outstanding Hindi play *Aadhe Adhure* by Mohan Rakesh, where the characters - all members of a family - suffering from angst, sense that something is amiss in their house, yet find fault with each other and struggle to get fulfillment in a meaningless world. As the title of the play suggests, we humans are fundamentally incomplete. This incompleteness often pushes us to attempt to complete ourselves through relationships, achievements, belongings, fame and other socially important structures. Void, emptiness, unease, meaninglessness, angst, depression are all manifestations of the FUNDAMENTAL UNHAPPINESS of human existence.

Another manifestation of our basic unease is our yearning for order, structure, patterns and predictability. All that helps cover our unease. However, it also limits our freedom. Paradoxically, while we humans may strive for freedom, we achieve it, along with anxiety. James Park has cogently described the correlation between freedom and angst:

> *"When we confront difficult choices, are we anxious? Perhaps freedom 'creates' anxiety because difficult decisions that require us to exercise freedom awaken our spirits and uncover our repressed existential anxiety.*
>
> *If the exercise of freedom releases **angst**, this might explain why we sometimes prefer to **escape our freedom**: Refusing to make choices protects us from existential anxiety."*

The brilliantly made American film *The Truman Show* directed by Peter Weir, written by Andrew Niccol, has shown how Jim Carrey, playing the character of Truman Burbank, chooses freedom and the uncertainty that comes with it, over his artificial yet secure world created by a television serial producer without his knowledge. When Truman comes to know about his artificial existence as part of a TV serial, the producer tries his best to entice him with the comforts of a predictable and secure, but artificial world. However, Truman prefers freedom and steps into the real world, which is full of uncertainty, to the applause of the watching audience. He thus celebrates his humanness. The film symbolically shows many of us similarly trapped in the *comforts* of our artificial worlds, far removed from ourselves, refusing to step into the real world as authentic individuals. Indeed, sensitive people who are able to feel their inner unease are more authentic, and by the same token, more human. As long as we are successfully cut off from our inner condition, we have still not lived in the real world. Even before you reach anywhere closer to FUNDAMENTAL HAPPINESS, this aspect of fully acknowledging our basic pain is a very rich experience, and takes our lives to a different level.

I feel so trapped in life!!!!

We think we are free. But do we understand freedom?

The more we forcefully depend on various external factors, situations, relationships, possessions, achievements, positions, the more we are trapped in life.

It may sound strange but we are all trapped in our social, economic, political, religious and other structures. Only if we face ourselves authentically will we be able to recognize this.

Imagine yourself without all this; it could be unnerving.

But doing that courageously brings autonomy and real freedom.

Once you have freed yourself, you do not have to shun any occasion, acquaintance or act that you deem to be enjoyable. Then you start enjoying all those from a different level. You do not cling to them. You actually enjoy even more for there is no fear of losing what you have. It could be a great idea to treat whatever good you get from the external world as a bonus.

Do not crave for anything. You can be fundamentally happy or be in state close to FUNDAMENTAL HAPPINESS.

You, then, do not need anything more. If anything enjoyable comes your way, and enjoying that is within your moral parameters, go ahead and enjoy. Now you have become morally responsible for your choices and therefore you can enjoy them far more than ever before.

All of you would have heard or read the story of Victor Frankenstein, the doctor who created a monster. There are about 42 versions of Mary Shelley's original novel. I have seen the 1993 TV version, produced by TNT, which features Randy Quaid as the monster. This adaptation of Mary Shelley's tale features Patrick Bergin as Victor Frankenstein, a doctor, who uses a laboratory to grow a human being (Randy Quaid) from his own cellular material. Though sensitive and intelligent, the rebellious human is driven by a murderous rage against his creator, compelling him to destroy everything that the doctor holds dear. This adaptation introduces a psychic link between Victor and his monstrous genetic offspring. One analysis of this version could be that the monster was nothing but the reflection of the doctor himself, or more particularly, his inner malaise. The doctor was running away from the monster much like we trying to run away from the monstrous suffering inside us. And, the monster was able to catch up with him everywhere, even in the freezing Arctic. Finally the doctor surrenders, embraces the monster, uttering his last words: *"I will help us both"* and the two take a plunge through the frozen ice embracing each other and go down the ice cold sea. It was only when the doctor surrendered and embraced his suffering that he found peace. This was yet another portrayal of our basic condition and how we enhance our suffering trying to avoid it. We find peace only when we fully acknowledge our suffering. This was a cinematic projection; you don't have to die to find peace. You can cherish every moment of life while embarking on a journey towards FUNDAMENTAL HAPPINESS.

> THE MORE WE FORCEFULLY DEPEND ON VARIOUS EXTERNAL FACTORS, SITUATIONS, RELATIONSHIPS, POSSESSIONS, ACHIEVEMENTS, POSITIONS, THE MORE WE ARE TRAPPED IN LIFE.

More recently some interesting aspects of spirit in humans was depicted in *Life of Pi* an American adventure drama film based on Yann Martle's 2001 novel under the same name. Directed by Ang Lee, the movie shows Pi trapped on a life boat with a tiger for many days on the high seas. My analysis of the story is that the tiger is a reflection of the monster within Pi, like we have this monster within all of us. In times of acute distress, the basic human condition often gets awakened and triggered; much like Pi discovered the tiger on a life boat. Pi was able to make peace by confronting and embracing the tiger. He admitted that the presence of the tiger helped him to survive in those conditions for so many days, which he might not have, had he been completely alone. He recognized his spirit and survived. His existence became richer. It is interesting to note that both in *Frankestein* and *Life of Pi* the inner suffering or malaise is shown as a monster which is calmed with an embrace. Then peace descends. In much the same way, if we recognize our spirit and are in touch with our deeper selves, we could be free from our inner suffering.

The 2009 Bengali movie, *Antaheen* (The Endless Wait) directed by Aniruddha Roy Chowdhury, beautifully depicts the emptiness or void felt by all the lead players Radhika Apte, Rahul Bose, Aparna Sen, Kalyan Ray and Sharmila Tagore. They all find something missing, they look for completeness, yet they are not sure whether entering a new relationship or restarting an old one is the answer. The tentativeness of human existence has been well captured in the movie. They are all waiting for something, yet they do not know what. They are all in an endless wait.

This reminds me of *Waiting for Godot*, an absurdist play by Samuel Beckett, in which two characters, Vladimir and Estragon, wait endlessly and in vain for the arrival of someone named Godot. Godot's absence causes a lot of angst and despair. They claim he is an acquaintance but actually do not know him. They also acknowledge that they would not recognize him if he does arrive. To keep themselves engaged while they wait, they talk to each other, eat, sleep, argue, sing, play, exercise, exchange hats, and even contemplate suicide – anything to hold the unbearable silence at bay. Godot never comes. Godot may not even exist. But the condition of the characters waiting for Godot, is much like most of us. Many of us could be similarly waiting for our Godots. That is very much the problem with humankind; we are either in the future, waiting for something, or we dwell in the past. Future causes anxiety and past causes depression. And, then we blame others. The trick is to be in the present. That is the magic proposed by Tolle in *The Power of Now*. Stay in the present moment. The very next moment, this will become the *past*, so move to the next moment, which is now the present moment. And, the best way to do it is to connect with your inner self, feeling your body and inner energy. Tolle has identified our body as one of the portals for spirit. Do not reject the body, he suggests.

The basic human suffering:

What if I say that, for most of us, the basic human condition is a sum total of the pain of meaninglessness, depression, fears, anxiety, and despair?

You will strongly disagree.

You will insist that you are truly very happy.

You will list out many aspects of your life that keep you happy, except for some quirks here and there. Others might agree to the basic unhappiness due to feelings of void or despair but will blame their circumstances for it.

But realizing this is the first honest step towards discovering the FUNDAMENTAL HAPPINESS within you.

It is true that our circumstances make us happy or sad. We must realize though that our circumstances are forever changing. The change they affect to our feelings is transient too!

The so-called happy situations do not last that long. Think of the happiest moment that changed your life. For how long did a dream job or a fairy tale relationship or a good house keep you elated? I am not being a pessimist. A pessimist has a list of reasons why he is not and cannot be happy.

Instead, I am saying, we all have a right to be happy.

We must savor happy situations.

That said I am only making you aware that you will need a continuous string of so called happy occasions to conclude that you are happy and content.

Many are plain lucky or actually able to *create* these happy moments for themselves, for a larger part of their lives.

Many of you will not agree with me. I can understand that.

The choice is yours. But realizing this is the first honest step towards discovering the FUNDAMENTAL HAPPINESS within you.

Notice how humans inflict suffering on fellow humans.

We torture, murder, rape, in the name of sect, religion, or geographical allegiance.

We hurt each other every day in smaller ways and justify it!

If you accept this, you will accept the FUNDAMNETAL UNHAPPINESS lying at the core of human existence. On a regular basis we embarrass, humiliate, cheat, scheme against, taunt, unfairly target, shout at, bad mouth, discriminate or put down fellow human beings with relative ease.

This is how FUNDAMENTAL UNHAPPINESS manifests itself, which some of us sense and others blame or deny.

What if we felt a hint of the FUNDAMENTAL HAPPINESS, within us? Would we have put others down, or hurled hurts at them? No! We would possibly still compete, strategize, or take strict action, but all such actions would be humane. But it is not so. This shows us the basic inner condition of a vast majority of human beings.

In subsequent sections, I have dwelt more on how the manifestation of this human condition can differ from person to person and also how denial is stronger in some than in others.

If you find it difficult to accept that we are fundamentally unhappy beings with an undercurrent of depression, meaninglessness, void, anxiety with tentativeness residing deep within us, then just pause for a moment and think about boredom. All of us use this term *boredom* very casually and take steps to try our best to not get bored. In the next section of this book, I attempt a detailed elaboration on boredom and how we often deal with it.

Whew!!!!
So much to do in my " Free Time"

4

Party
Gym
Movies
Cricket
Gardening
Hiking

BOREDOM

B oredom – a common experience of most people. From time to time.

But we have found ways of not confronting boredom.

We quickly divert our minds.

We occupy ourselves with activities.

Some important and useful.

Others, mere distractions like partying, unwinding, having fun.

We also find comfort in following to a time table packed with schedules. In other words, our time is fully structured.

Here is a paradox! We schedule our *free time* slots, then pack them with activities called *fun*.

What would happen if we did none of these things?

Is it possible to live with boredom without a struggle?

On a more serious note, boredom can be unnerving if left unchecked. How do we find out?

My own experience tells me that lurking beneath boredom is the painful, but fundamental, human condition. Most of us have never been exposed to our inner condition, but all of us can sense it. So we always run away from boredom. Our mind is trained to pick early warnings of an impending confrontation with our innermost condition. Boredom is one of them.

There are others too, like loneliness.

If boredom is nothing but a manifestation of the basic human condition, then courageously facing it, submitting to it, embracing it, would be wise.

In other words, instead of running away from boredom, you welcome it.

Be honest as you do so. Check if we really *are* confronting it.

Watch out! We human beings possess a very manipulative mind. It is quite possible that as we pretend to face boredom by avoiding a distraction, our mind has already escaped into some other happy, distracting thought.

One can try to honestly face boredom keeping the mind still. But at the same time, we should not fight with the mind. If thoughts come, witness them passively, as an onlooker, instead of engaging with them.

With practice, one can learn the difference between observing one's thoughts from a distance and becoming the thoughts themselves. The steps you could follow for this appear in a subsequent section of this book, titled: *'Step by Step towards FUNDAMENTAL HAPPINESS.'*

Once we truly face boredom, it is possible that it opens up more uneasiness and tentativeness inside us. The process can make us really uncomfortable. If it does, you are on track. But do not fight boredom. When I say, "face boredom" I am not suggesting a

I embrace you Mr. Bore... Cheers!!!!!

combative posture. I repeat what I have mentioned in an earlier paragraph: submit to it, embrace it. Just be with it.

The more we focus on what is going on inside us, the clearer we are that pain is fundamental inside us. Just focus inwards without any analysis.

We might notice that at its basic level, our existence is painful.

And this pain we successfully kept suppressed through distractions.

We realize that we humans are Fundamentally Unhappy.

It is this profound experience from within which opens up the possibility of a peep into unexplained bouts of joy. This joy is also within us; it is also fundamentally there. But it is beneath the FUNDAMENTAL UNHAPPINESS. To be able to feel the FUNDAMENTAL HAPPINESS within us, and reach that level of this unexplained joy, we have to first face and accept the FUDAMENTAL UNHAPPINES, also embedded deep within us.

No one can take it away from us. How this can be possible is detailed in subsequent sections of this book.

The conventional normal life as such has nothing to offer.

We overlook this fact.

We try to find meaning by doing things that can be considered important, purposeful, or interesting.

Indeed most of us succeed in leading such *purposeful* lives except for those stray moments of despair which we manage to overcome.

Probing deep within ourselves, we might notice, to our horror that all the activities however interesting or captivating, gradually fail to enthuse us.

We quickly look for newer alternatives.

Could this be because in reality there is no lasting meaning or purpose in whatever we do?

If we have the courage to be authentic, and squarely face the fact that the material world has nothing to offer to us in tangible and durable terms, if we have the courage to face the fundamentally dull and bland nature of human existence, if we do not run away from the mundane reality of our existence, we might discover the fundamental joy of existence.

Interestingly, this joy is not derived from anything *real* in the external world. It is uncaused, and is just there for us to savor. It is actually within us. It is FUNDAMENTAL HAPPINESS.

> ONE CAN TRY TO HONESTLY FACE BOREDOM KEEPING THE MIND STILL. BUT AT THE SAME TIME, WE SHOULD NOT FIGHT WITH THE MIND. IF THOUGHTS COME, WITNESS THEM PASSIVELY, AS AN ONLOOKER, INSTEAD OF ENGAGING WITH THEM.

Unfortunately, we have mastered the art of keeping ourselves focussed away from fundamental joy within us. We are therefore cut away from it. We have created so many barriers through our *needs, ambitions, addictions, compulsions* that we just do not know what existence is like at the basic level. Unfortunately, nature has its own rules. There is no short cut to this fundamental joy within us.

If we do muster up courage to deeply look inwards, free of all external diversions, we will first have to witness a pile of pain, despair, meaninglessness, anxiety. Only after we fully feel the pain, do we have the chance of feeling our inner joy.

At that stage we will not need external props in life.

To know more on how to go about this, read on.

5

All HUMANS
SEEK
FULFILLMENT

A ll humans want fulfillment. This, perhaps, is the single most striking difference between humans and other animals. Domesticated animals – dogs, for example – are known to seek affection apart from seeking to satisfy basic needs. However, both humans and animals, strive to satisfy their basic needs. Humans, who can easily meet their needs for food, shelter, and clothing, are truly fortunate while the unfortunate ones, unsure of their next meal, or survival, struggle against odds, which are very often man made. Then we move on to higher needs like security, affection, and warmth. We do various things to acquire these. We can move to even higher needs, like recognition, self-esteem and the sort. The overwhelming human need, as we can see, is towards overall satisfaction and fulfillment. That seems to be a part of the human DNA. I remember that in my discussions with my psychiatrist, Dr. Gupta, my stress was on lack of fulfillment, and an all-encompassing sense of meaninglessness.

Earning money, having relationships, receiving successes, making acclaims, taking vacations, acquiring assets – are some of our higher order needs. Unfortunately, everything that we do to fulfill them belongs to the external world.

A bit of ponder will show us that none of these needs can give us lasting fulfillment.

These higher order needs are important, but not what offers lasting fulfillment.

At the job,

With noble intentions,

You find success.

And enjoy it.

No problem in doing that.

But try to seek lasting fulfillment or meaningfulness of existence in this success, and a problem arises – you will make yourself want success always and in all tasks you perform.

Even if you are successful, the deeper question will stay: is this lasting fulfillment? What is the ultimate meaning of life?

We have no answers and we reach a dead end.

The edge. Beyond this edge is the pit we all carefully avoid.

It is scary to have no answers, we feel unsure, unsafe without a haven. We do not venture near.

We learn to distract ourselves far before reaching this edge by looking for other means of fulfillment.

But then, there are the sensitive, inward-looking ones amongst us. The fundamental question overwhelms them. Looking for an answer takes them over the edge - into the pit.

And the long journey of struggle and pain begins.

I'm ready for the path of growth

Once inside the pit, we cannot force ourselves up and out of such a place.

These sensitive, inward looking individuals amongst us, who land inside the pit – do we term them *unfortunate*? On the other hand, those who successfully avoid reaching the edge, are they the *lucky ones*? If you read on, you might discover that reality could be just the opposite – those who go over the edge, have within them, both, the opportunity and the motivation to go beyond. All they have to do is to stall all struggles and discover the FUNDAMENTAL HAPPINESS within.

But watch out! To give up the struggle and not clamber to safety does not come easy or naturally to us humans.

Our minds are wired to provoke us to always reach for security.

Once inside the pit , we are badly stuck.

There is no return.

Instead, if you can face the darkness of the pit with courage and adopt a posture of surrender you might discover the joy beyond the fundamental human unhappiness. All world religions propose the common idea of *surrender* – but for sake of simplicity, I suggest you first accept your present state of being.

That is surrender.

As you go through this book, the significance of *surrender* will get further clarified.

You need courage to do this.

The same courage that you mustered up as an adult, and entered the swimming pool for the very first time.

You watched others float easily on water while you gathered courage to do the same.

Your trainer demonstrated it for you.

You tried it.

You were able to experience the truth that struggling in the water actually increased the chances of drowning.

You saw that you could actually float if you surrendered.

You tested this kind of surrender and the learning was confirmed.

Unfortunately, the spiritual plunge does not seem the same. You cannot *see* others gently float on the water of suffering once they have given up the struggle. You just have to believe and trust what those who have done it narrate as their experience.

James Park has described this dilemma through another image:

> *"Perhaps an image will help to clarify the meaning of this surrender: We are dangling down a dark*

*well on the end of a rope. The well is the pit of our existential despair, anguish, absurdity, & guilt. The rope to which we cling is our last hope of being able to pull ourselves out. After struggling for many hours (years, decades), we finally conclude that we cannot climb out of the pit of existential nothingness. All we can do is **let go** of our last hope of self-sufficiency.*

*But when we release our grip on the rope, everything changes: Instead of falling to destruction in the pit, we float gently out of the well. To our surprise, we discover ourselves beyond dread, forlornness, & exile. We are lifted into peace and at-homeness when we **stop trying to attain it. The result we could not achieve by our efforts is granted as a gift.**"*

This imagery makes immense sense. But you have to unconditionally believe in it. No one can demonstrate it to you. You cannot *see* someone actually float out of the well of despair.

Interestingly, the possibility of finding FUNDAMENTAL HAPPINESS within is also embedded in the human nature of going for higher needs. Abraham Maslow developed the *Hierarchy of Needs* model in 1940-50s, and the Hierarchy of Needs theory remains valid today to understand human motivation, management training, and personal development. According to Maslow, humans start with basic biological and physiological needs, then move up to safety needs, further up to need for belongingness, esteem needs, and finally to self-actualization. Indeed, the need to fulfill one's own unique potential (self-actualization) is what I wish to emphasize here.

The need for self-actualization possibly propels us. It makes us transcend other lower needs to seek the FUNDAMENTAL HAPPINESS within us. Those of us who do not feel the dullness, meaninglessness and the mundane nature of human existence are hopelessly stuck at the *Belongingness and Love Needs* level. I am not suggesting that you don't fall in love or nurture relationships. A bit of self-search, may throw light upon the strong sense of *addiction* to these needs. Enjoy your relationships, but check whether you are clinging to them. This desperation is a signal that deep within us resides the FUNDAMENTAL UNHAPPINESS that we carefully avoid. We pretend to not recognize. We fear to face. And we hunt newer relationships to fill up the fundamental incompleteness we feel deep within. Possibly, it could be a better idea to move up, instead. Those who migrate to the *Esteem Needs level* may too question their basic purpose in life and seek to move further up. In a later chapter I have written about existence at *one level below FUNDAMENTAL HAPPINESS.*

Please study the diagram in the following page. It appears what Maslow describes as Self Actualization could roughly correspond to the FUNDAMENTAL HAPPINESS that I am referring to, though it need not be an exact fit.

Let's dwell more on the need for belongingness. If you approach your relationships from a higher level that is closer to FUNDAMENTAL HAPPINESS, chances are that such relationships would be more of mutual respect, cooperation and understanding, and hence, lasting, rather than the clinging *romantic* type, likely to break. The key question to ask is whether you are trying to satisfy some void within while sticking to a relationship. You need courage and authenticity to be able to accurately respond to this question. This is a key question facing an increasingly large number of people, particularly in urban settings and in the developed world. People are getting into a series of relationships. Each relationship begins in a fairy tale, romantic style, but does not last long enough. Before long, either or both (most often, eventually both) move into new relationships. Marriages do not last. This is also supported by the liberal setting that is available in most urban cultures today.

Maslow's original vision as seen from the perspective
of Fundamental Happiness/ Unhappiness.

However, I do support the liberated stance where couples find the freedom to break away from a relationship that is not working, or where one partner (often the female) is suffering abuse. It is far worse to remain stuck in a relationship due to societal, moral or other pressures. The same can possibly also be said of people who keep changing jobs.

The moment of concern is when one starts to find a relationship boring or lacking the initial spark.

When that happens, we blame each other for it.

The more fundamental question that actually needs to be authentically addressed is,

'Why am I bored?'

'Why is my partner bored?'

'What is the source of this boredom?'

'Is FUNDAMENTAL UNHAPPINESS rearing its head?'

If you had found *profound meaning* in life through this romantic relationship, it is possible that you had used the relationship to suppress the basic condition of FUNDAMENTAL UNHAPPINESS.

If so, then the relationship was merely a cover up, and was bound to fail sooner rather than later.

I could not agree more with James Park when he states *"That 'true love' is the solution to our Existential Predicament is one of the strongest illusions of the Western world. It will not die easily. Perhaps only continual disappointment will convince us **that love cannot fill our existential emptiness."** I am certain that by the word 'love' Park is referring to romantic love. Romantic love has a chance only if it transcends into a mature relationship of mutual respect, space, companionship and sharing. That the clinging kind of relationship is only a ploy to fill our own void is a truth we all have to face. Romantic love has all to do with *satisfying my need* and nothing to do with the partner. Each partner is actually using the other to cover his or her fundamental dissatisfaction and emptiness. Unfortunately cinema and popular culture have placed romantic love on a very high pedestal.

Many of you will possibly dismiss me as a spoiler, a joy killer. I am only stating what I consider the fundamental truth. Honestly questioning the origin of a squabble with your partner usually leads to a truth – either both of you or one was not kept happy or *entertained* enough by the other. We focus a lot on keeping ourselves happy. That is one of the usual strategies through which we keep our inner condition at bay. In that situation, a romantic pair puts pressure on each partner to keep the other *entertained* most of the time. One of the standard romantic dialogues is: will you keep me happy?

I emphasize on this aspect of romantic love because we humans often remain stuck at this level without moving beyond. We are actually programmed to evolve and grow; and unknowingly restrain ourselves. Ken Wilber in his book *A Brief History of Everything* has given an exhaustive account of the evolutionary journey of human consciousness. He builds his framework around fulcrums or steps in the evolution process. Wilber describes nine such steps, from Fulcrum 1 to Fulcrum 9 quoting extensive research.

At birth, according to Wilber, the self is in fusion with the sensorimotor world. The infant's identity is fused with the material dimension. Around 4 months, (Fulcrum 1: Sensoriphysical) the infant will begin to differentiate between the physical sensations in its body and those in its environment. This differentiation completes itself by 5-9 months. But the emotional self is not yet established and is fused with those physically around the infant, particularly the mother. Somewhere around 15-24 months

(Fulcrum 2: The birth of the Emotional Self) the emotional self begins to differentiate itself from the emotional environment. Some researchers call this 'psychological birth of the infant.' At the next level (Fulcrum 3: The birth of the Conceptual Self) the self is no longer exclusively identified with the emotional level. It begins to transcend that level and identify with the mental or conceptual self. This is the beginning of the representational mind. From age 6-7 to 11-14 (Fulcrum 4: The birth of the Role Self), one develops the capacity to form mental rules and to take mental roles. The child learns to take the role of the other. The next level sees transcending of the conventional roles and rules, and gaining freedom from them. Wilber calls this Fulcrum 5 (The Worldcentric or Mature Ego).

What Wilber calls the next level Fulcrum 6 (Vision-logic), is of particular interest to me, and the readers of this book. The Self, at this stage, represents an integration of body and mind in a relatively autonomous self. Wilber has quoted John Broughton's research and summarizes: "First of all, the self at this stage is *aware of* both the mind and the body *as experiences*".

After reading Wilber I realized that this is the level where many of us suffering from depression, meaninglessness, anxiety, or void exist. This is also the level where your consciousness has already achieved a degree of evolutionary growth. You are already at a higher level of awareness, and therefore ideally placed to make the next move upwards, instead of repressing yourself downwards.

To elaborate this further, I would like to quote Wilber:

> *"One of the characteristics of the actual self of this stage (the centaur) is precisely that it no longer buys all the conventional and numbing consolations – as Kierkegaard put it, the self can no longer tranquilize itself with the trivial. The emergence of this more*

authentic or existential self is the primary task of fulcrum – 6. ...

The existentialists have beautifully analyzed this authentic self,...

...this is classically the home of existential dread, despair, angst, fear and trembling, sickness unto death – precisely because you have lost all the comforting consolations!...

But the interesting point is that the centaur, by all orthodox standards, ought to be happy and full and joyous. After all, it's an integrated and autonomous self, ... Why, by all standards, this self ought to be smiling all the time. But more often than not, it is not smiling. It is profoundly unhappy. It is integrated, and autonomous, and miserable. ...

This is a soul for whom all desires have become thin and pale and anemic. This is a soul who, in facing existence squarely, is thoroughly sick of it. This is a soul for whom the personal has gone totally flat. This is, in other words, a soul on the brink of the transpersonal." (A Brief History of Everything)

The most significant transpersonal stages proposed by Wilber are all stages beyond Fulcrum – 6. Just beyond this level lies what I call the level of FUNDAMENTAL HAPPINESS, and the intermediate levels close to it. The most exciting learning I acquired from Wilber, is that while you are suffering, you are on the brink of the transpersonal! The reason why I brought Wilber in this section, along with Maslow, James Park or Eckhart Tolle is that all that they have stated in their writings point to the same direction, even though their beliefs or orientations could be different. In the case of Park and Tolle, it is based on their own experience.

What I write is also based on my experience.

> **LIKE A REFLEX ACTION, OUR MENTAL CONDITIONING PULLS US DOWN, MOVING US AWAY FROM PAIN. YET THE PATH IS THROUGH THE PAIN.**

A key aspect of Wilber's *"vision-logic"* or *"existential"* state is that *"the mind and body are both experiences"* of the Self. Further in this book you will read my thoughts on being *conscious of your consciousness*. James Park has described it as *"moment of vision"*. This state is one of the most significant insights in my own journey towards FUNDAMENTAL HAPPINESS. We use our mind to experience so many things. Can we experience our mind? Not many, other than the inwardly sensitive ones, may fully understand this question. The reason is simple: we are so integrated with our mind, that we cannot see the mind as distinct from ourselves. We are the mind. Yet through spiritual exercises, described by me in a step-by-step approach in a subsequent section, it is possible to experience our mind. We can observe our mind, like we are able to observe different parts of our body. Notice your existence. Be aware at all times that you exist.

My thrust in this section of the book is on the nature of human consciousness to evolve and grow. Literature and research show that evolution of consciousness results in more aware and enlightened human beings. Along this path of growth, there will be struggle - uncaused depression, meaninglessness, and anxiety or void. These could be some manifestations during this growth process. This underlines the experience of many philosophers, as also my own, that the way out of misery is further growth. Like a reflex action, our mental conditioning pulls us down, moving us away from pain. Yet the path is through the pain.

Trying to avoid it actually increases the pain.

6

STEP BY STEP TOWARDS FUNDAMENTAL HAPPINESS

I will now attempt to describe how to go about it. The steps are simple, but the results can be profound. More than anything else, you will soon be able to appreciate that being on the journey is more important than the end point. It is not a *start-to-finish* rush. Do not get too obsessed with the end point. As you grow more stable in your journey you begin to relish the richness of a new life. Even the very advanced enlightened persons on earth consider themselves still on the journey. That is the beauty. Some of these aspects will appear clearer in the next section of this book. So, with patience read on.

Step1

Begin with asking yourself whether you are ready. If you consider yourself to be *happy* and *contended* with the way you are, there may not be the need or motivation to get into the posture suggested by me. Please don't be under the impression that you will get *thrills* out of asking deep questions. The journey towards FUNDAMENTAL HAPPINESS has nothing to do with new or additional *thrills*. If you are looking out for new excitement in life, you perhaps need to ask a deeper question. You may wish to probe what within you drives you to look for endless excitement. If you are able to honestly answer that question, it could well be a good starting point.

Consider facing the basic dissatisfaction in life. It is possible that you focus on the circumstances or other people as the main reason for your unhappiness. Amongst those who are suffering from a basic dissatisfaction with life, there could be two possibilities. One possibility is where people suffering are probably still focused on the circumstances or other persons as the main reasons for their unhappiness. You need to take a close look: is it possible to get out of the circumstance? Is it possible to significantly change it? Is it possible to stop dealing with the persons responsible for your misery? Often you are faced with the choice of walking out of a situation or a relationship. That could be the best decision, sometimes. Importantly, this has to be your call. Beyond this you still have to question yourself. How much of your misery lingers that cannot be further assigned to any situation or person? Have you reached a dead end? If you cannot honestly blame anyone else, you are possibly at a dead end. Here you might well be ready for Step 2. The second scenario could be for those who are already faced with fundamental questions about life and the purpose of existence with no answers. People in this scenario already know that at the fundamental level there is nothing to be happy about. Everything is dull and meaningless. This could cause depression, anxiety, and feeling of emptiness or a sense of void. If you are one of such persons, I consider you fortunate, for you are most ready for Step 2.

I'm on a Holiday

Step2

Be ready to take a *holiday* from your usual lives. If your job profile allows it, take a *holiday* without absence from work. This will allow you to focus within yourself. Externally you will be the same. If you are too occupied, you need to decide on how to get that *holiday*. This applies equally to those who are not professionally employed but are too pressed for time - housewives leading packed lives with responsibilities and pressures. If you are overly burdened, at least in the initial stages, you may find it difficult to focus within and look for those subtle messages. Those readers who are on the edge and witness an existential dissatisfaction will be able to understand what I am suggesting here. They may look forward to this holiday. Many of you would wonder how long this holiday would be. Well, it could be as short as one week or long enough to last a few months. As you fall into the groove, you will be able to go back to your *normal* life, but with a completely new orientation and an internal shift. You will continue to notice internal changes within yourself. You will have now embarked on a journey.

Step 3

For those who are witnessing unease of varying degrees and kinds, the best way to start is

- To courageously face your basic condition,

- To focus all your attention within and,

- To feel your discomfort squarely without distraction.

Your mind will want to fight, distracting you with the external *causes* behind the unease. Do not fight it. Instead, observe it. Observe your suffering as well.

The depth of your painful suffering may surprise you. But do not get distracted by that.

Focus, instead, on the pain itself.

You will learn quickly the art of observing. Many of us are keen observers of the world around us. But we are, perhaps, not so good at observing ourselves. You can master the art of observing yourself, by gradually shifting focus to what is going on inside you. Initially your attention will typically go towards your mind.

We humans are like that – too defined by the mind. You should be able to reach the stage where you notice your being, your consciousness.

We are conscious of so many things. Are we conscious of our consciousness? Are you aware that we have the power to be aware?

To be aware of our consciousness is an extraordinary experience. It is actually the start of a new state of being.

If this sounds too baffling, then may be, my own experience will help. I have had these extraordinary moments when I was aware of myself in a heightened way since I was a teenager –

much before I actually got caught in depression and suffering. It would arise as a sudden surge in consciousness while, say, I was attending the school assembly. It used to be so unnerving that I would have to do something to immediately distract myself. Subsequently, when my inner malaise got fully exposed in 1972 and I lapsed into depression and anxiety, these moments used to be the most dreaded ones for me. I remember getting into such moments, for instance, while walking on the road, and I would get so startled noticing my presence that I would start running, just to take away my attention. At a very deep level, it was as if I could sense another existence within me, which was separate from my *normal* physical self I was familiar with. It would usually happen when I was alone, not surrounded by many people, in an open place or a completely new place. Interestingly, after my own paradigm shift in life, when I became more aware and had the first few glimpses of FUNDAMENTAL HAPPINESS, these moments of being conscious of my consciousness were precisely when I would feel the bouts of joy arise from within. I can fairly assess and say that today I identify more with that other self, who is real, rather than the familiar physical self. I'd like to again stress on the need for subjectivity and sensitiveness. Being too objective, can make us emotionally obtuse, and miss out on these outstanding moments. You can also miss these moments if you are emotionally hyper about situations external and refuse to peep within yourself. These moments come so subtly that you are most likely to miss them in the midst of the huge noise surrounding your lives.

> **WE ARE CONSCIOUS OF SO MANY THINGS. ARE WE CONSCIOUS OF OUR CONSCIOUSNESS? ARE YOU AWARE THAT WE HAVE THE POWER TO BE AWARE?**

If those currently leading contended and *happy* lives, decide to seriously take an inward journey, in the way I have described, they will be surprised to see how much of unease they carry within at the very basic level, overlooked in our noisy and active lives. The appropriate term for this would be existential uneasiness. As one continues with this practice, one may notice a pronounced increase in the level of one's unease, starting to feel it during the usual daily routine.

We might question getting into something likely to spoil our happiness. Well, what we presently experience is happiness at the circumstantial level, and what we might get eventually is happiness at the fundamental level – at the level of spirit. But please remember, the decision of this has to come from within you. This is not a scientific experiment with predictably accurate results.

Here we are dealing with human consciousness.

It is about crossing a hump. Once you are on the other side, everything falls into place, and you become a more authentic person closer to FUNDAMENTAL HAPPINESS.

Things look much simpler.

Should you take that leap? That is the key question you need to address.

Those suffering from existential depression and anxiety may have the motivation and opportunity to do so.

As I carefully sensitize you about considering what you do, honestly speaking this is not very different from what yoga teachers ask of us. In a true yoga session you are required to focus inwards. Otherwise you are only doing the physical exercise. You might as well go to the gym for that. Physical exercise is necessary and good for health. But right now we are discussing a spiritual exercise that could be good for our spiritual journey.

Step 4

As you stabilize yourself at Step 3, you need to develop a regime for your inward journey.

I can share what I have practiced. Every night I calm my body down before finally going to sleep. I make sure there is no distraction of television, mobiles, or bright lights in my bedroom. Then I lie in a reclined position on the bed. I do not lie flat. It is not necessary for the room to be pitch dark. I prefer to be able to look around.

Once in the reclining position, allow your body to fully relax.

One at a time, focus on each part of your body.

Start with your toes upwards till you reach your head. You can repeat this process a few times.

As you do this, feel the liveliness in each part.

Pause briefly at each part of your body as you shift focus up to the next. Observe the stress and uneasiness, but do nothing about it. Just become mindful of it.

Gradually focus on your breathing. Observe the rhythm of inhalation and exhalation.

If you are suffering from depression or other psychic pain, focus on that pain without trying to analyze it.

My own experience is that sustained but passive attention to the pain almost dissolves it.

In some time you might experience an inner energy through your entire body.

Tune in to that inner energy. You are quiet, you are relaxed, and you are very still.

Yet you will be able to feel the energy within. Relish this energy.

Stay in this state for about 30 to 40 minutes.

You may feel like closing your eyes and tend to fall asleep. Before you actually do, you can either change your posture to the way you usually sleep or choose the reclined posture.

Months later, you may experience some flashes of joy while in this stage. If you have come this far, you are well onto your spiritual journey. Next day when you wake up, you may find a peace you have not experienced before.

I hit upon this method thanks to a combination of suggestions made by Eckhart Tolle, and utilized my own experience during the autohypnosis sessions I had attended many years ago under supervision of Dr. Gupta as part of treatment of my stubborn depression. I am not suggesting that autohypnosis is necessary for you. I just incorporated the stance from that methodology and found it helpful in my own journey. Autohypnosis has other elements designed for treatment, which I do not practice.

Having just started your journey, you might experience heightened pain. I experienced it when I took the dive. For those of you who may currently be under medication, here is what I'd like to share: to stay functional, I continued with my medication for a week or so, until I was able to notice major positive changes in me. That prompted me to discontinue medication completely. Thereafter, I discovered that I was *joyfully* noticing my pain. Within months I could see the pain gradually dissolve. These steps can also be followed while under medication.

Once you start feeling better, you could consult your doctor and discontinue the medication. Probably he will taper the medication off.

Step 5

These steps are not enough.

You will need to attempt a major shift in your orientation towards life.

Question your attachment to things in the external world.

Not just possessions.

Not just the attachment you have to the car, wealth, property, or other material things.

Question also your attachment to position in society or workplace.

Question your attachment to achievements, biases, judgments, and beliefs.

Can you see yourself without these?

You do not have to give up these things. Many wise people have attained salvation having actually given up everything in life. Prince Siddhartha is believed to have given up his royal life to become Gautama Buddha. Probably that hastens the process. I do not really know, and do not recommend it. I do, however, recommend questioning attachment, questioning all that you do to keep yourself happy or distracted.

Step 4 may bring you to some basic unease that you were overlooking before. When it does, you can question all that you do to escape this uneasiness for most of the day.

Remember the chapter on Boredom? Now is a good time to honestly face and question your strategies to keep boredom away. Now is a good time to welcome and embrace boredom. When you do so, life might suddenly look meaningless. You might question: *'What the hell am I doing?'* You might get that strong urge to distract yourself and get back to the *normal* state. I suggest you stay with meaninglessness, unease and disquiet or anything else that you may feel. Have the courage to face it. Trust me. You will come to no harm. This is nothing but a spiritual exercise. Just as we strain our bodies in physical exercises to remain physically healthy, we need to do these exercises for spiritual wellbeing.

EGO
The Monster within

This step requires a major shift in our stance, attitude and orientation. A big beast living within us is our ego. If you take a close look at our attachments, you will notice that most of them satisfy the need of the ego.

Questioning our attachments and attractions, gets our ego to substantially diminish. This focused attention, devoid of ego, or compelling attachments, is what is called the posture of *surrender.*

In our day-to-day lives, surrender is possibly a negative word. It has connotations of losing out, giving up, or accepting defeat. The obstacle in the way of surrender is our ego. And, when we are not surrendered, we have resistance within. It is this resistance that causes pain while surrender opens the way to peace and joy. Surrender is not weakness. It is a manifestation of wisdom.

It is okay to be alarmed at the thought of giving up attachment to things. You need not actually give up everything, just don't be defined by them or cling to them. It could lead to some insight. This insight works well for those who are already suffering from depression, anxiety, sense of despair and void. Having lost the taste for most things in life, they have almost given up. For them, surrender is just one step away. Merely facing their condition honestly would be a posture of surrender for them. The surrender will not cause further gloom. Trust me. You'll be pleasantly surprised. But first, give up. Surrender.

If you are alarmed at the thought of giving up attachment to things, stay with that alarm.

If you wonder how you can be happy by giving up all the things of joy, you have not yet faced the truth.

This could typically be the question facing all those who are leading *contended* lives.

> **FORGIVENESS IS FOR YOUR OWN SAKE: FOR THE SAKE OF LASTING PEACE WITHIN. IF YOU THINK YOU HAVE DONE A FAVOR TO SOMEONE BY FORGIVING HIM, YOU HAVE ACTUALLY NOT FORGIVEN.**

At some stage you might realize that you are right now living an artificial, fake life supported by several props and safeguards that prevent you from living a realistically full life. Therefore, people who are currently *satisfied* with their lives are perhaps not yet ready to make that shift. It is important for you to decide when you can be ready to do so. At some stage, probing questions about life may face you. You may consider then taking the leap. If you think you will miss the ego driven world of complete attachment, please be patient.

In subsequent sections of this book I have dwelt on topics like

The Spiritual CEO, Spirit and Wealth Creation and Brand Loyalty. Moreover, I am a living example of a person, a CEO, who did not quit his job.

Step 6

As you move deeper into the spiritual realm and a deeper self, you will need to strengthen your stance by giving up many things that we are involved in on a regular basis. Once you have reached Step 6, you will appreciate what I am suggesting and will have no difficulty in giving up some. For sake of simplicity and better understanding I have summarized them below:

i.   **Taking revenge.** Given a chance we all try to get even. It could be small petty things or, at times, life's mission. The urge to get back and retaliate is tempting, in spite of the fact that it creates the maximum negativity in us taking us away from spirit. We live under the domination of our mind and ego. It hugely satisfies the ego if we are able to get back at someone. Oh! It's so rewarding. Behavioral science has an acronym - NIGYSOB for Now-I-Get-You-Son-Of-a-Bitch, which may sound very satisfying when we have avenged someone. However, we pay a huge price, and it takes us away from FUNDAMENTAL HAPPINESS. This fact is completely missed out and ignored. Forgiveness, on the other hand, does just the opposite. Forgiveness brings peace that we may not have fathomed earlier. Please do not confuse revenge with the appropriate action necessary in a given situation.

As a boss you might have to take strict action against a recalcitrant employee. A person disruptive to society has to be booked and locked up. There is a difference between revenge and appropriate action for disruption. The key difference is the reason you are taking the required action. Revenge is an action taken on a person who troubled you personally in the past. Your ego gets satisfied now by taking him on. But when you take appropriate action for disruption by a person, your ego is out of it. That is the correct thing to do. Your egoistic *Self* should not be in the action. It might appear confusing, but the difference between the two approaches is stark. I can recall one example from my personal life. I once had to work around the exit of a very troublesome director from the board of a company. He had humiliated me several times. But the reason I got his exit was because he was not sincere in his approach. He did not keep the best standards of governance in mind. He was largely driven by his personal agenda. He was being obstructive, actually becoming a hurdle in the orderly functioning of the company. Until finally, all board members accepted that it was time for his exit. The job of taking the necessary step came on to me. I did the task without seeing it as a victory, and without any sense of glee at having gotten even with someone. That sense was crucial. I must admit that the temptation of enjoying the process was nudging me. Instead of fighting that temptation, the better way was for me to acknowledge it and be aware of its destructive value. One has to be very truthful to oneself; to be sure the negativities of revenge are purged within. Whether you have successfully kept your ego out or whether you are just taking an action, while also enjoying it, is a question you have to honestly address. In either case, the winner or loser would be you. Finally, please remember that forgiveness is for your own sake: for the sake of lasting peace within. If you think you have done a favor to someone by forgiving him, you have actually not forgiven.

The moment you walk over to someone and tell him that you have forgiven him, you have played with your ego and have moved further away from spirit. The act of forgiveness comes from a higher state of existence, from self-awareness and wisdom. Revenge comes from the mind and ego. Forgiveness comes from the being.

nigysob!!!
but at what price?

ii.   **Carrying old baggage.** We actually love to not only hold old grudges but also nurture them. We may not go so far as taking revenge, but we create a monstrous baggage of negativity, which we might carry all our lives. We cherish our baggage like any other valued possession. Have you ever wondered why we find it so tremendously difficult to shed old baggage? Probably because we try to derive meaning out of it. For many of us, the baggage may be the sole reason for existence; we attach undue value to it. We spend time and energy preserving this baggage. We seem to derive sustenance from it. By now it should be occurring to us that in this entire process we are feeding our ego. It is the ego, which attaches a high value to our baggage. And, we cannot let go. If you have reached Step 6 of my suggested regime, you would probably be trying to identify the baggage you carry. If you are honest you will realize that the uppermost question might be: what do I live with if I shed this baggage? Cursing someone for something or some event that happened ages ago becomes not only a favorite pastime, but is also self-serving. So, today if you try to shed this baggage, you might be giving up a cloak that has helped you cover up the true human condition, the inner malaise, from which all of us seem to suffer. Since you are already at Step 6, you might have the courage to face yourself with the baggage gone. You might discover, to your surprise, how light you feel, and how you carried a heavy burden for no reason for all these years. You will also realize how unhappy you were all the years you held on to this heavy burden.

The choice was always yours. Also, you are today a more authentic person, well on track towards spiritual wellbeing. If you are honest you will appreciate that the biggest resistance to shedding baggage comes from the imagined specter of giving up your reason to exist! But that is an illusion – it's actually our inner condition rearing its ugly head. There are countries that seem to exist solely on the basis of old baggage. Some have shed the baggage, embraced the presumed enemy and moved on.

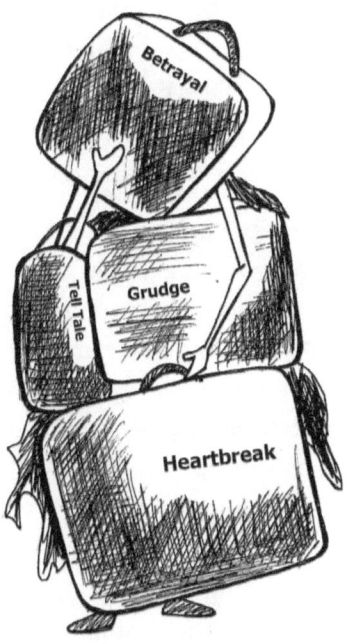

Ahhh...maybe I'm carrying a little extra baggage.

iii. **The 'I' syndrome.** Many of us don't miss the opportunity of talking about ourselves. When at it, we never speak about our vulnerabilities or failures. The focus is on our successes in life. It is easy to identify people who are full of themselves. But we need to take stock of our own selves too. Whenever you feel this urge to speak about the great things you have done, pause. Observe what is going on inside, and give it up. In the first few attempts you may experience discomfort. Try to stay with it. Staying with any inner discomfort, and just observing it, is a very powerful spiritual exercise. Each time we consciously refrain from bragging about our own successes, we rise in spirit. We are on track towards FUNDAMENTAL HAPPINESS. This practice is not to be confused with situations where you need to strategically make known your abilities and achievements – in your workplace, to your superiors, sometimes subtly to your work team. Once again the honest question is: *'Have I acted from the need of my ego?'* Interestingly, while it is quite easy to judge and identify people who are full of themselves, it might not be that easy to come to the same conclusion about our own selves.

iv.   **Staying with a hurt ego.** Our egos get hurt easily. However, some of us get rattled more easily than others. Egos get hurt for useless and unimportant matters. While driving, for example, another impatient driver may be honking behind us. We react in different ways – give him way and be done with it, or deliberately not let him go past until he overtakes, making an ugly gesture as he goes past. Again, there are some who will just ignore the gesture. Others will try to catch up with him and give it back. We hear of many instances of road rage, some even resulting in death. Staying with a bruised ego is a helpful exercise. The example above is an excellent situation where we could let go. With more spiritual practice, such events will no longer affect you. Before you reach that level in your spiritual journey, you need to accept that your ego is hurt, and silently observe your pain. Dealing with a bruised ego, on one hand, and standing up for your rights or the good of society on the other, are two different things, not to be confused with each other. Again, the moot question is: *'what prompted me to take that stand? Has my ego played a role?'* Also, staying with a hurt ego, as an observer of that ego, is not to be confused with a sulking posture of self-pity. Self-pity is a pastime of the ego and it helps to conjure up a false sense of self. Some people are capable of living their entire lives in self-pity. They seem to be peaceful, at least externally, are often not destructive, but they lead miserable lives, far removed from FUNDAMENTAL HAPPINESS. And, they cannot create a joyful climate for their loved ones.

v. **Hurting others.** In our day-to-day life, we often hurt others for silly, unimportant reasons. It goes without saying that there could be situations where you need to take firm action. In a subsequent section titled, The Spiritual CEO, I have underlined how, if you are a person closer to FUNDAMENTAL HAPPINESS, you will have the ability to pull up a person, or take someone to task, without actually hurting him. If you are unnecessarily hurting others you are working from your ego. People who are sarcastic, insolent and loud get easily identified, and then avoided by many. It is ironic that, apart from hurting others, they are themselves unhappy and in complete denial of it. If you ask them they are usually *fine* about their state of happiness. It is easy to identify such people in society who are, by their very nature, sarcastic and intemperate. They often hurt others. On fewer occasions, we may be doing this as well, but it is often overlooked. We are capable of being fundamentally happy so we should not look at others to be the cause for our happiness. And we should also not be the cause of unhappiness to others. It is very easy to get hurt and hurl hurt at others. As we move up the spiritual ladder, we can make ourselves immune to unhappiness caused by others, and yet give a lot of happiness to others. It is a win-win situation.

vi. **Catch yourself complaining all the time.** We often complain – about things or situations. Yet we notice many others, in the same situation, who do not complain. I can say for myself: I am usually the first to get fidgety and restless if the boarding call for a flight gets delayed. Even when the delay is not further affecting an important meeting say, my impatience builds and I find myself making frequent enquiries about the causes of the delay. First I used to justify this stance. Then I shifted my orientation, got more aware of this impatience and questioned it. It could be a good exercise to actually observe what is going on inside you whenever you have the itch to complain about something. There could be important issues we face in life where we need to take a principled stand. We should be able to take it, but not from the ego. Next time you complain about this or that, observe and judge for yourself and question if your ego is at play. I acknowledge that many good things happen in society, laws get changed, reforms happen because someone has dared to complain. Raising your voice against injustice is a completely different issue. What I am drawing attention to is our propensity to keep bickering about small things mostly in our personal lives.

vii. **Fast pace of life.** For many of us the sheer pace of life could be reduced. We do not realize how we race ahead in life. If we take a closer look we may find us always ahead of time. One good practice is to stay focused on each bit of work that we are doing at any point in time. Brushing our teeth, putting on our clothes, having breakfast, catching the transport – didn't seem to need our complete focus. Or did it? During my earlier years, I have driven from home to office, and then realized that while I was driving, my mind was everywhere except on driving. Apart from this being a posture away from spirit, it was plain dangerous! Can we start the practice of focusing on every bit we do? At work, when you have tea, take time out to enjoy that tea. Feel and relish every sip of the tea. You deserve that. Many of us have the experience of doing some repetitive, boring work, bordering on drudgery. I remember having to often sign every page of a bulky pile of papers – nothing hugely important, but necessary. Often I would sign them grudgingly, constantly eyeing the number of pages left. I realized, that way I was only increasing my unhappiness. I was building resistance. And, resistance is the source of most pain. Instead, how about, taking each paper joyfully, feeling it, putting your signature neatly on each paper, focusing on each bit of the job, without rushing to the end of the work? Chances are that the total time taken will only be marginally more. I would surely have the advantage of possibly making the task in hand less painful, and also position myself in a spirit-ready posture. In other words, I have been more present with the task at hand. There are numerous such examples of how we rush all the time. Deteriorating handwriting, not being able to replicate our signature, are similar small examples of our being ahead of time. Always staying ahead of time creates anxiety. Conversely, always living in the past can bring about depression and forlornness. Being in the present moment, and noticing presence all around is an extraordinary spiritual practice. I remember a family friend with an extreme habitual practice of staying ahead of time: she would move the home calendar to the next month almost a week before the end of the month! By being in the present, we can also avoid temper tantrums. Whenever I have lost my temper, I have felt hugely ashamed of myself. Staying with that shame instead of justifying the temper loss helps.

As you embark on your journey you will come across postures and practices that enhance your spiritual life, which you can share with others. These are powerful tools and you will have much creativity at your disposal. There will be pitfalls, ups and downs. Please do not condemn yourself for not being able to adopt the correct posture, or taking time to deal with your ego or any prejudices. Remember, we are all human, and we have been conditioned to think and react in particular ways for years, and generations. So give yourself a chance. What is required is commitment, commitment to a new life. This shift will not happen if you attempt from an *'OK, let me also try this out'* mindset. Something deep within has to tell you that this is the only way. You have the records of experience of many others who have traveled this path. Before you embark, make sure you are convinced. Remember you are free to reject this completely. The choice must be yours. All you have to say is *'If I decide to take the plunge, I will do so with full commitment.'*

You may sense disturbing messages emanating from within – an integral part of the journey. I have witnessed several such signals during my journey. You will get used to it. I did. I was suffering and didn't know anything about this new shift in life. The severity of the depression and anxiety appeared as a physical sign of feeling unwell. I once went to a cardiologist thinking I was seriously unwell. The doctor ruled out any disorder. I insisted. Can you beat this? He asked me to consult a psychiatrist for I could be suffering from anxiety! No diagnostic aid, no matter how advanced, can actually detect our FUNDAMENTAL UNHAPPINESS. It can only catch some of the physical manifestations, like higher heart beat rate, higher blood pressure etc. which can be the result of any stress in our lives, existential or circumstantial. If you feel your inner condition strongly and you visit a doctor, you are more likely to be sent to a psychiatrist.

However, it is certainly an excellent idea to keep yourself under expert medical watch. If you notice some not-so-familiar upheavals, by all means consult a specialist to rule out any cardio-logical or any other medical situation. Such a situation could co-exist without it having anything to do with your shift in life and the journey you embark upon. But the last thing that I would want is mistaking a real signal about a heart condition or some other ailment as a spiritual message. It is always a good idea to err on the side of caution. Mistaking a subtle message from the level of being as a symptom of a medical problem is safe. You can have yourself checked and rule it out. But the opposite – where you dismiss an actual symptom of a physical disorder as one of the subtle spiritual messages – can be a disaster. Forget spiritual journey, even otherwise you would have heard about situations where one may have just missed a faint warning signal of an impending heart attack.

7.

LIVING ONE
STEP BELOW
FUNDAMENTAL
HAPPINESS

s it really so simple?

To let go?

To surrender?

To find peace?

My suggestions may rattle you, but I will say it again: we need to shed our overwhelming attachment with the physical, external world.

I assure you that you can still enjoy the good things in life.

The beauty is that as you move closer to FUNDAMENTAL HAPPINESS, you realize that all the things that we crave for give us transient pleasure. Once you are more a person of spirit, you will appreciate and enjoy many more things in life.

Without any attachment!

Broadly there are two kinds of attractions: those that appeal to our sensory perceptions (touch, feel, taste, sound, sight), and those that we believe will give us peace of mind and security (possessions, wealth, position, power).

Sensory perceptions are only a pleasure of a moment. Have your favorite chocolate. How long does the joy last? The chocolate does get over! Then we tend to want more unless more compelling concerns like maintaining low cholesterol or a good figure creep in.

Or take sexual contact - the experience craved most by humans.

Can you hold on to the climax and make it last long?

From my male perspective, it lasts as long as a flash.

I do not suggest abstaining from chocolates or sex.

In the subsequent chapters, I propose, in fact, that the best way to enjoy any sensory aspect of life is to enjoy every moment of it. But I also suggest let each moment pass. Don't try to cling to a moment. When the present becomes past in the next moment, then dwell in the new present moment. That keeps us clear of the urge to have more and more.

As Eckhart Tolle says, "be present" all the time. Osho too suggests that being aware of every moment of sexual contact could be a way to spirituality in *From Sex to Super Consciousness*.

All that is important is to be aware of what goes on within us when we crave for something, and what it actually gives us.

We also look for *long term* satisfaction and security. We sure must make secure our future. And possession of wealth does give a warm, secure, feeling.

The problem arises when we do not know how much is enough, and get addicted to asking for more and more.

There are successful entrepreneurs who have, through their hard work, contributed a lot to the community and have also created a fortune for themselves. But I wonder what prompts some of them to build massively scaled residences larger than public office blocks. Once we reach these stages, we are removed further away from ourselves. The more we want, the more we head towards the danger zone of falling into the dark pit. Yet, ironically, once we are inside the pit of suffering, we have that great chance and motivation, with the right stance, of floating out of it and enjoying FUNDAMENTAL HAPPINESS.

> THE BEAUTY IS THAT AS YOU MOVE CLOSER TO FUNDAMENTAL HAPPINESS, YOU REALIZE THAT ALL THE THINGS THAT WE CRAVE FOR GIVE US TRANSIENT PLEASURE. ONCE YOU ARE MORE A PERSON OF SPIRIT, YOU WILL APPRECIATE AND ENJOY MANY MORE THINGS IN LIFE.

I have to be true about the fact that very few people would truly and completely be in the FUNDAMENTAL HAPPINESS state of being. And these are the spiritual gurus of our world. Our distant past tells us that most founders of religions were themselves enlightened beings and had truly reached FUNDAMENTAL HAPPINESS. In fact this state could have well been their permanent state of being. Unfortunately their preaching is mostly misunderstood and their followers are trapped in the rituals and form. You would have heard about many of our contemporaries, enlightened beings like Sri Aurobindo, Ma Anadamayee, Osho. Based on their discourses it is easy to guess that they had reached that level of being. More recently, you may have witnessed enlightened persons who dress and look like us, seem to be living modern lives not very different from us; they are persons we can identify with. Indeed spirituality has reached our living rooms, iPads, and Facebook! Eminent people like James Leonard Park, Eckhart Tolle, Deepak Chopra and many others - I suspect most of them are either fully redeemed and enjoy FUNDAMENTAL HAPPINESS, or keep witnessing that state very often.

Indulging in spirituality is the full time occupation to these experts. I fully understand the difficulty in maintaining the posture of surrender and remaining spiritually inclined all the time as well as going about the demands of daily existence and life's struggles. If you are too busy or have too many things to do, you have no time left to look inwards. The posture of surrender may get lost.

I strongly recommend all readers of this book to take a brief holiday from daily life, for three to six months or more depending on where you are in your spiritual journey. Take a close look at yourself and adopt the stance that I have explained earlier. Those who are actually suffering from the existential kind of depression and anxiety, this is your chance! You are just a few steps away and could redeem yourselves from suffering and taste FUNDAMENTAL HAPPINESS. All of you must taste FUNDAMENTAL HAPPINESS at least for some months. You might discover to your surprise that suffering and joy are two sides of the same coin. As you focus on your pain, you might be at a stage where the pain is suddenly replaced by bouts of joy. After years of suffering when I stopped running away from it, this has been my experience. It is like a swivel door: you can move in and out of depression, anxiety, or meaninglessness.

As you hold your posture of surrender, you might taste a glimpse of FUNDAMENTAL HAPPINESS. If at this stage you choose to go back to your previous *normal* lives, you are most likely going to slip back from FUNDAMENTAL HAPPINESS. You can start all over again, as many times you want. But you would be a more *aware* person by now.

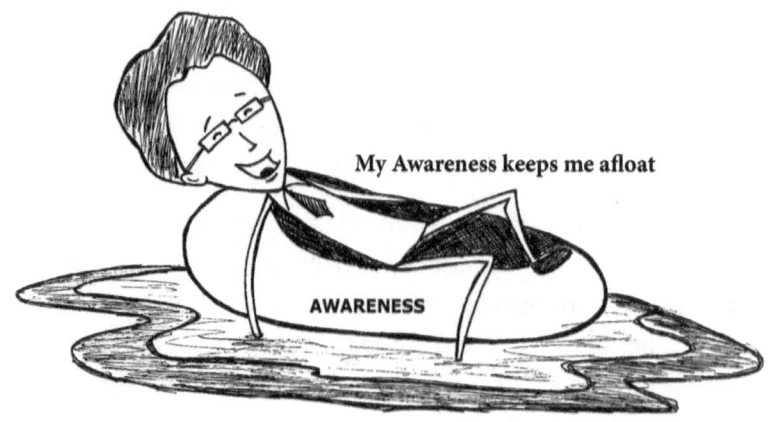

My Awareness keeps me afloat

AWARENESS

In your regular, busy schedule, you may find it difficult to maintain your presence all the time. But your awareness will ensure that even as you slip from FUNDAMENTAL HAPPINESS, you do not go down all the way to the pit of suffering.

It is possible to continuously live a life *one step below FUNDAMENTAL HAPPINESS*.

Your awareness will work as a solid platform, which will not allow you to sink further below.

The basic human unease may occasionally tease you.

It will remind you that it is there.

But it will stay in the background.

Welcome it and embrace it warmly even if it threatens to overcome you. It will actually melt away!

Being an aware person, you will never again try to run away from the malaise.

That is the trick.

We suffer because we fight our malaise, resist it and try to free ourselves from its grip.

In fact life with the basic human suffering as a silent partner that keeps gentle company but does not disturb your orientation or take you over completely can be greatly enriching. You become a deeper, more sensitive person. You worldview changes completely. You begin to observe the external world from a *higher* level. So you do not try to cling to it anymore. You are able to calmly face downsides in life. Your professional life is likely to improve. Your problem solving skills take form of a higher order. Others notice something special in you and look up to you, without knowing anything about your elevated existence. The cherry on the cake is that whenever you find the time, you can go deep within to enjoy the reassuring glimpse of FUNDAMENTAL HAPPINESS! There are times, when in the midst of a problem you can feel the joy deep within. While externally you deal with a problem, internally you feel the flashes of joy! Can you believe it? Imagine! You will never get fully identified with any problem. There will always be a space between you and the problem at hand. Isn't that a great state to be in?

The biggest gift of living a notch below FUNDAMENTAL HAPPINESS is increased creativity. This kind of perspective and the worldview could give you the ability of lateral thinking. It won't surprise me that writers, film makers, composers, artists who have produced masterpieces have deeply experienced the basic pain of existence and may have, at some stage, moved closer to FUNDAMENTAL HAPPINESS.

Please remember that reaching the level of FUNDAMENTAL HAPPINESS is not a straight-line journey that has a start point and an end point.

The journey to FUNDAMENTAL HAPPINESS, itself is satisfying, energizing, educating and vastly revealing.

Of course like any other process in life, there are ups and downs in this process as well.

You are bound to sometimes reach close to FUNDAMENTAL HAPPINESS, and then slide back.

You may even feel disheartened and give up the journey at some stage.

But you will realize that if you stay on course, your cravings for many things you consider very dear in life could diminish; yet you can still enjoy them, but without a strong sense of attachment.

That is really the trick to stay in the journey towards FUNDAMENTAL HAPPINESS.

The diagram in the following page gives a visual impression of what I am trying to convey.

I have to say about myself that I was in the surrendered state for close to a year, when I repeatedly experienced FUNDAMENTAL HAPPINESS. Pressures from my professional life increased and it was difficult for me to hold on to the posture. That is when I discovered the beauty of existing just below the level of FUNDAMENTAL HAPPINESS. It has helped me immensely in my leadership positions, including my current role as a CEO. One of the subsequent sections in this book is titled, The Spiritual CEO.

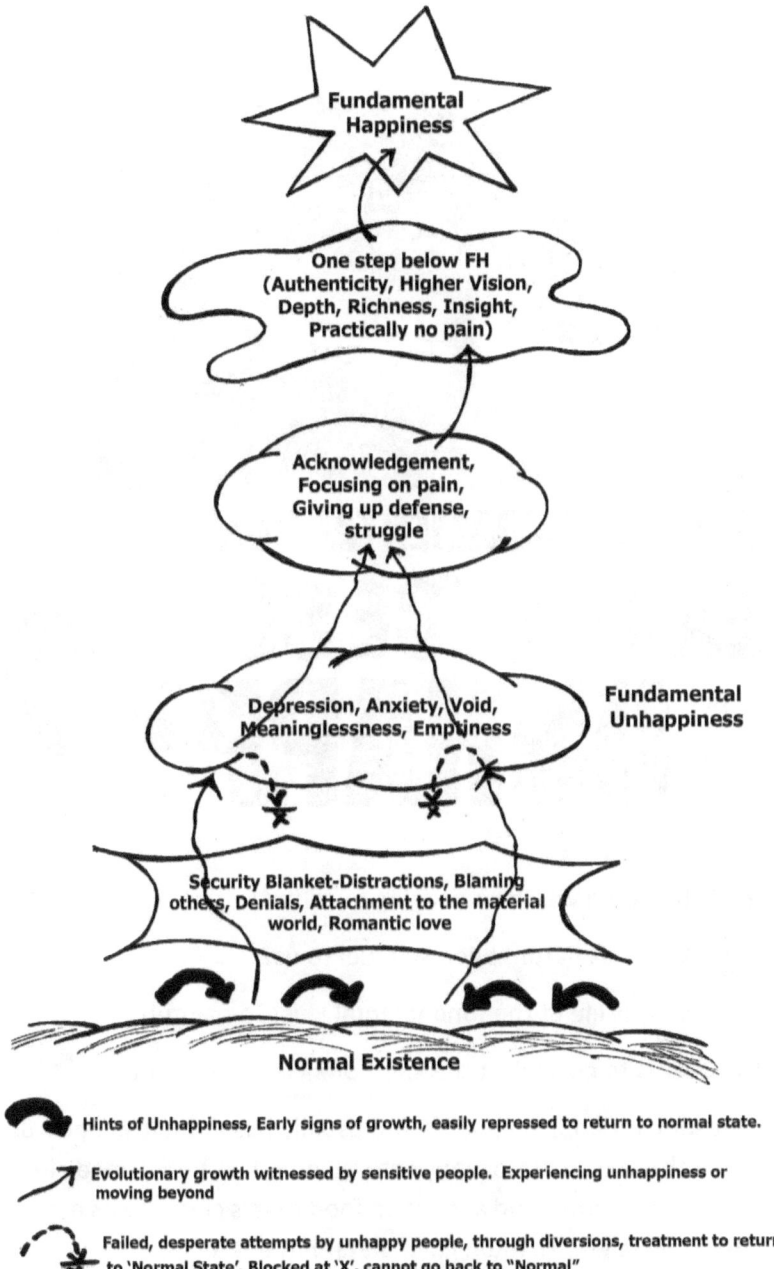

Fundamental Happiness

One step below FH
(Authenticity, Higher Vision,
Depth, Richness, Insight,
Practically no pain)

Acknowledgement,
Focusing on pain,
Giving up defense,
struggle

Depression, Anxiety, Void,
Meaninglessness, Emptiness

Fundamental Unhappiness

Security Blanket-Distractions, Blaming
others, Denials, Attachment to the material
world, Romantic love

Normal Existence

Hints of Unhappiness, Early signs of growth, easily repressed to return to normal state.

Evolutionary growth witnessed by sensitive people. Experiencing unhappiness or moving beyond

Failed, desperate attempts by unhappy people, through diversions, treatment to return to 'Normal State'. Blocked at 'X'. cannot go back to "Normal"

8.

WHY IS FUNDAMENTAL HUMAN
EXISTENCE SO
UNHAPPY?

T his could well be a nagging question.

Why has nature been so cruel to us?

Why is life at the fundamental level so painful?

This seems to go against the spirit of all laws of nature.

If we look around, we find nature usually has in-built safeguards. That is the reason for so many natural remedies, herbal medicines, naturopathy cures, and a focus on food that is closer to its natural form: coarse grains, multi gain, dietary fiber etc.

Then, why has nature been so harsh with us?

We have to ask another question to be able to address the

question at the head of this section: Was basic human condition intended to be so painful? Now, that is a hypothetical question and at best, the answer could be correspondingly tenuous. Nevertheless, let me attempt an argument.

My guess is that the present condition of human existence has come about after years of evolution. I doubt whether the very first humans on this earth would have strained themselves, like we do now, for seemingly useless things like fame, ego, position, attachments, or wealth. Early nomadic man was probably doing much like what animals do even now. He was at the basic level of the human need hierarchy – food, shelter and protection of the progeny. Looking at him from our present day perspective, we would conclude that it was probably a pathetic human existence then. I am not sure. Yes, humans suffered insecurity then too. Do we not suffer from insecurities even now? Now our insecurities are hidden and masked under our egoic presence. Probably the earliest human enjoyed the bliss of life. Over centuries of evolution, we have lost touch with ourselves and have accumulated a lot of pain within us.

Most probably we humans, being endowed with enormous intellect, were able to find ways of *entertaining* ourselves. Beyond the basic needs of life, we were able to create other needs for ourselves. Later we got completely driven by the mind-ego combination. The extraordinary gift of mankind – the very sharp intellect – also turned out to be a source of a lot of pain. And, the combination of mind and ego has proved to be almost lethal!

Intelligence, sensitivity, compassion and power to introspect are some unique qualities humans are endowed with. We also carry negativity in the form of ego, jealousy, vindictiveness, and propensity to carry baggage. The sum total of the positives and negatives that we humans are endowed with has, unfortunately, prevented us to *just be*.

We have lost our presence.

We have used our intelligence for creating and discovering great things in this world.

But the same mind, in association with our ego, has also made us crave for more and more.

With the help of our mind, we can escape the present and project into the future – into some imaginary world of bliss.

We run after that.

Beyond a point, we are so focused into the future that we do not notice that we are running away from ourselves too.

Or we brood about the past. We remain stuck in the *glorious past*.

Living in the past or in the future are both painful.

We are just not able to remain in the present.

We just cannot *be*.

Our sharp intellect, ability to project to the future, or reflect on the past, coupled with our desire, with almost matching ability, to extract everything from life have made our lives so painful. The collective human consciousness has accumulated pain inflicted upon itself over centuries of unstoppable craving and striving. The suggestion is not that we shed our intelligence and imagination. Our mind is a valuable tool available to us. It should be at our disposal. Unfortunately, instead of being a soul that manifests itself as a body and mind, we have become primarily a mind that also has a body and traces of soul.

The net result is that the *normal* human being today is full of anxiety, depression, void, and meaninglessness.

The more we strive to find meaning in this world, the more we suffer from emptiness.

One important difference between man and animal is that no animal is as aware about its inevitable death or non-existence as humans are. Animals protect themselves from danger through reflex action. We too act on reflexes on many occasions. Yet, we are fully aware of our inevitable death. This is an added burden humans have had to carry since the beginning of existence. The consequential fear of death too had to be repressed and pushed aside. The totality of all this fuses together as FUNDAMENTAL UNHAPPINESS at the very core of what is human. FUNDAMENTAL HAPPINESS, ought to have been our natural state. It is also at the core, but it is locked deep within. It is not available to us in our natural existence. Probably nature did not intend to structure it this way. We humans are extremely gifted. Unfortunately with all our abilities we have also created a lot of pain within us. It is possible to enjoy all the gifts we are endowed with – intellect, perception, imagination, compassion, ambition, and courage – after we have acknowledged our FUNDAMENTAL UNHAPPINESS, and tasted our FUNDAMENTAL HAPPINESS.

> **UNFORTUNATELY, INSTEAD OF BEING A SOUL THAT MANIFESTS ITSELF AS A BODY AND MIND, WE HAVE BECOME PRIMARILY A MIND THAT ALSO HAS A BODY AND TRACES OF SOUL.**

Yet, this human suffering provides an excellent opportunity and motivation to move up the evolutionary ladder to higher consciousness.

Another way to look at it is that we humans were probably destined to evolve. I am not certain if animals have the capacity to similarly evolve and grow in consciousness. By virtue of our reflexive reactions, we unfortunately put barriers to this evolutionary growth. Perceptive and sensitive persons reflect on the early signs of growth in human existence and, therefore, sense the embedded pain. They must move up. There is no other way. Other *normal* humans are either not as sensitive, or actively divert their attention. They are stuck at their level of existence.

Interestingly the biggest problem faced by mankind today is not that this pain has been created over centuries, but the fact that this pain is mostly denied and wrongly blamed on others and ascribed to circumstances. If we can impart a little awareness and acknowledgement to this pain, life would become richer, deeper and insightful. You are then automatically on a journey. You move towards FUNDAMENTAL HAPPINESS. It is no longer so much about precisely reaching FUNDAMENTAL HAPPINESS than relishing the journey itself. You suffer as long as you, knowingly or unknowingly, struggle against it. Once you give up the struggle and let go, you find peace.

> **HUMAN SUFFERING PROVIDES AN EXCELLENT OPPORTUNITY AND MOTIVATION TO MOVE UP THE EVOLUTIONARY LADDER TO HIGHER CONSCIOUSNESS.**

Humanity has accumulated a lot of pain. Thanks to the immense mental potential at our disposal. Suffering the accumulated pain offers us humans the unique opportunity to transcend it and embark on a journey towards FUNDAMENTAL HAPPINESS. I think this is the key difference between human life and any other life form like dogs or monkeys. So, it would be a shallow thought to conclude that we humans are an unfortunate lot for having to fundamentally suffer so much. The same fundamental suffering opens up the possibilities of growing and moving to a different level of existence. I think that is great news.

Can only FUNDAMENTAL UNHAPPINESS be transcended?

I have written extensively about transcending our FUNDAMENTAL UNHAPPINESS to seek FUNDAMENTAL HAPPINESS; that has been the central theme of this book. But humans have the potential to use any other suffering, even circumstantial suffering, to move towards FUNDAMENTAL HAPPINESS.

The trick is to focus on your suffering alone, and not the reasons behind the pain.

We are faced with distress and real reasons in our circumstances that cause the distress.

The reasons could be people, sheer bad luck, and unfair treatment in your family, workplace, or almost anything. The first reaction naturally is to protect yourself from the source of this pain. You must do that.

You owe that to yourself.

Having done that, many of us stay stuck there, probably cursing their fate, cursing people, and indulging in self-pity.

In the process, we create baggage.

You could refer back to the section where I have elaborated on how we cling to our baggage. The irony is that it is possible to dump the baggage to lighten us, and move on.

Many people do so and, in the process, they themselves benefit the most.

What I propose is, instead of merely moving on and brushing your suffering aside, how about trying to just observe your pain?

How about focusing all your attention on your suffering, without any analysis of how or why it happened, who was responsible, how awful some people are, and giving up the temptation of indulging in self-pity?

Believe me; the very first step is difficult – because, our mind and ego come up as obstacles.

The mind just loves to go to the *root-cause-analysis*. Ah, that is a familiar phrase, particularly in doing post mortems during any system failure! And, what better system is there than our mind?

With practice and some courage and truthfulness, it will be possible to cultivate this art of just observing your pain: feel yourself internally as you suffer and notice what it is doing to you.

Observe your body: is it tensed up?

Is your breathing pattern different?

Just observe your heartbeat.

If you can adopt the correct posture, you might notice a significant loosening up of yourself.

This posture is *surrender*. You might even find a disconnect between the cause of the suffering and the suffering itself.

Now you are on a journey!

Maintain the posture as you go along.

9

THE ART OF DOING NOTHING

Having come so far, you will be able to appreciate the fact that we humans are quite smart at ensuring that we keep ourselves *busy* most of the time.

Even our *free* time is adequately structured.

I have talked about this in Chapter 4 titled Boredom.

It will be easy for you now to understand that from the perspective of spiritual development, we need to master the art of doing nothing; to just allow ourselves to be.

If this posture is doing something to you, pause and observe yourself.

Notice what goes on within.

If you wonder how you will get time for such luxuries amidst a very busy life, you will be surprised to discover countless such opportunities. While waiting for your daily transport, when caught in a traffic jam, while waiting at the airport, while traveling, when in a queue, waiting your turn in a hospital – there would be numerous opportunities for you to just be.

While doing nothing, there are a few things that you can actually do. Tolle has described this technique in his *The Power of Now* whereby you observe things around you, without trying to analyze or understand them.

He talks about being a passive onlooker and noticing how things exist.

This works best when you are in a silent place.

Notice the silence.

Notice and appreciate the empty spaces between objects.

Notice and appreciate the empty space around the mountain

I have personally found this practice most powerful. In silence, possibly in the dead of night, notice the empty, vacant spaces all around us or between objects. Do not try to focus or analyze or give meaning. Just notice and appreciate. Also notice that you are noticing. You can then be conscious of your consciousness.

The mind loves to quickly give meaning to everything.

It is a mental exercise.

On the other hand, as you observe, if things appear meaningless, stay with the meaninglessness.

As you practice this spiritual exercise, you will be able to observe things with greater depth.

You may actually sense objects turning alive.

You will be able to notice their presence.

That is the crux – notice just the presence of stuff all around you.

Even a mundane, meaningless object that you observe might appear more alive to you.

That is the beauty of spiritual depth.

You see things with a different kind of vision.

Inanimate objects will appear to have life.

As far as other life forms are concerned, like trees, plants, animals, you will connect with them.

You will come closer to nature.

> USUALLY, WHEN WE SEE OBJECTS WE AUTOMATICALLY GIVE THEM A MEANING. TRY OBSERVING THEM IN THE BACKDROP OF THE EMPTINESS OR THE SPACE THAT HAS ALLOWED THEM TO BE.

I have a habit. I gaze out of windows of high-rise buildings, and notice other high rises occupy the space surrounding them. This is one practice that has helped me a lot. You can try the same thing with mountains. Usually, when we see objects we automatically give them a meaning. Try observing them in the backdrop of the emptiness or the space that has allowed them to be.

This emptiness we call space is endless. Objectively, it is easy to understand that space has no boundaries. Imagine the vastness of this emptiness that has allowed all physical entities to be. The space between you and the object closest to you is the very same space, which is accommodating the solar system. We call it by different names like *outer space*. When we master the art of gazing, you realize that it is the same space everywhere. We get a new insight and depth into what we have been observing otherwise for years. We tend to miss out the space, or we objectify it. For instance we have made the sky an object. Try visualizing it as just emptiness. As soon as we do that, it connects with the void within us and awakens the spirit. Even the space between the nearest object and us is missed; you can try and notice that.

Once you understand this spiritual stance, you can discover your own methods of connecting with the spirit and share it with others. It is an exciting story. But be careful of anyone trying to make you believe in the occult. I do not believe in ghosts or fantasies. They are as well the fictional creation of humankind to address the basic dilemma of human existence. Since we fail to understand the subtle messages that we keep getting from within, and we are frightened, we create ghosts and fairies. We have created a scary outer world to objectify our inner fears, which we could not comprehend.

I have placed a photograph on the next page. My office is in one of the high-rise buildings.

This is the view I get from my office window. I'd like to draw your attention to the two residential towers you see in the distance. Notice the greenery below. I developed a sense of oneness with these buildings. I did not see them as giant structures. Instead, I saw them in the backdrop of the vast open space and the sea beyond. I often sensed that I could pluck these buildings from the foliage and place them gently back. I could feel the buildings

turn alive. I could feel a living presence in the structures. The idea is not that you should attempt to see the same buildings and strain yourself into noticing presence. My experience is merely an example. Once you have progressed spiritually, you may be able to sense the presence in any object, say a chair in a quiet room.

What do we do when we go on vacations?

The usual, of course.

We pack all our time with sightseeing trips.

But do we really see what we look at?

Or do we just end up being very *busy*?

An enriching vacation would be to try doing nothing because our everyday lives are filled with activities.

Gazing is an example of doing nothing. Gazing at nature, gazing at the waves, mountains, the space between mountains, trees, plants, flowers, the flow of a river, the sheer vastness of the scene. Whatever type of place we are taking a vacation in, gazing at whatever we can observe is more enriching than rushing around and tick marking the number of places we have seen.

The richness of your *gazing* is more worthwhile than the list of places you see on a vacation. Have you observed a toddler looking around with a sense of awe? We all have a child within. If we reconnect with that child within and begin looking at things with awe, it could help us to connect with our spirit. That could be a good practice. We could then look at even ordinary things with awe. Look wondrously. However, the idea is to refrain from analyzing what we see. That is what we often do: quickly analyze or just look but do not observe. We may go to a lovely beach and watch the sun set, take pictures etc. But do we really *see* anything? Especially, when we have the capacity to make every sunset a new experience!

The art of doing nothing can also be well practiced at home, whenever you find the time. Please do not make it a task. The essence of it is *nothing*. And by creating time for it, you will have turned the *nothing* into *something*. Sit wherever you are comfortable, and just gaze at things around you in the room. Notice how everything is present. It helps noticing when everything is still and silent. You require a degree of inner sensitivity to be able to see objects around you with a new kind of vision. It is so subtle that you can easily miss it and lapse into the usual way of objectifying everything.

I remember once traveling to a hill station. We were two families together traveling in cars. In the middle of forestland, we had to stop and step out of our vehicles due to a minor hitch in one of the cars. It was daytime, but there weren't many vehicles on that road. As I stepped out, I noticed the deafening silence. As a city dweller I had been used to regular noise; I had forgotten what silence was. Sensing the stillness all around was deeply rewarding. My wife and another friend traveling with us, also immediately connected with the silence. We were in touch with our spirit. The experience lasted for about 6-7 minutes. It was an excellent moment during our trip to Mukteshwar; so close to nature. But I could not get another such connect there. These subtle messages get lost in the din of life.

There is a family friend who often travels from Delhi to his farmhouse in Chamba in Uttarakhand and stays there for months to take care of the orchards. Very often he is there alone, while his family is in Delhi. Being an artist by profession, he has shared vivid details of the scene there, the beauty, especially the complete silence at night. Once he described having sensed the presence of *someone* else in the room. He knew there was no one. Of course he did not believe that there was a ghost in the room. He smilingly said that he made peace with this *someone* and let him be. He was convinced that this *someone* was not there to harm him. However, he did notice a presence. I did not want to disturb the purity of his thoughts and so heard him out. I was tempted to tell him: that other person was only he himself! We can notice presence in wondrous ways. If I am not fully aware, and if I notice my own existence in a profound manner, I may project it to another existence. But I appreciated my artist friend's sensitivity in sensing what he did. He not only noticed it, he made peace with the presence. That gave him tranquility. He loves going to Chamba to spend some months there. He does not use spiritual language to express the experience, but obviously he has been able to connect with himself in the silence and has enjoyed hints of FUNDAMENTAL HAPPINESS. Some other person could have concluded that the place has ghosts, and probably destroyed his solitude. Whenever we have noisy company, we move away from spirit.

10.

RELIGION AND SCIENCE

I f you study most religious texts, you will find the basic human suffering mentioned along with guidance on how to be released from it to find lasting joy and peace.

Most religions resort to using symbols and mythology to simplify this to the masses.

Hence there is a fair degree of mythology that surrounds most religious texts of the world.

There is nothing wrong in simplifying texts using symbols or mythology as long as they take you on the right path.

My own belief is that religious texts have, over the years, been misunderstood.

As a result most followers have got trapped in the form and structure of the religions and are blindly following them as ritual without being anywhere on track towards the discovery of joy and peace, or what I call FUNDAMENTAL HAPPINESS.

So instead of staying simple, texts have got complicated.

However, the process that I have described to help stay on course the journey towards FUNDAMENTAL HAPPINESS can be followed irrespective of whether one is religious or not.

There could be problems if one is very deeply religious, because that hard creed itself could be a big external prop or crutch, and, as you would have seen by now, we need to discard all external support systems to truly adopt a posture of surrender.

Ironically just as deep religious beliefs can hinder the stance of surrender, a very staunch anti-religious position can have the same effect.

Strong anti-religious beliefs, the kind practiced by communists, can themselves become a creed.

Communists might claim that they do not believe in religion, but their dogmatic stand, by itself, works as a proxy for deep religious belief.

For them communism is just like a religion, and by that token I see hard-core communists as very deeply religious persons too. I have absolutely nothing against communists or deeply religious people.

This is a matter of personal choice.

The limited point here is that both these categories may find it difficult to adopt a posture of surrender. It may well be argued, why at all is surrender or seeking FUNDAMENTAL HAPPINESS necessary. Well, that is your choice too.

**Everything need not have a scientific reason or explanation.
Learn to just be.**

Science

It is good to have a scientific attitude.

A scientific mind helps us to understand many things in the physical world and enables us to objectively approach most problems.

Many of the daily comforts and conveniences we enjoy have been made possible by scientific research, backed by technology.

However, just as in the case of strong religiosity or rabid anti-religious stance, extreme objectivity can also cut you off from a possible helpful degree of subjectivity.

Sensitive persons will agree that we humans need to be subjective as well.

For, if we completely wipe out subjectivity, we deny ourselves so many subtle messages that emanate from nature or consciousness. We also surely miss many nuances of daily life. One can gaze at the furious ocean waves for hours.

Yet one cannot scientifically deduce why one savors it.

Similarly, a subtle note in a musical piece, a gentle twist in the notes might stir you up.

Science cannot explain why.

An outright objective person looking for a scientific explanation for every event is likely to miss the *relish* of these moments.

Everything need not have a reason or be explained through the cause-effect relationship. We ought to learn to let ourselves just be.

Complete objectivity does not allow this.

Unless we allow some degree of subjectivity, we might surely miss even the glimpses or hints of FUNDAMENTAL HAPPINESS as we embark on our journey towards it.

Yet, science is fully compatible with all that I am proposing in this piece. By training, I am first a physicist and then a management post graduate. I have often thought of an example that can stir us up, and is still fully compatible scientifically:

Take two spherical objects A and B separated by a distance of, say 10 meters. Now reduce the distance by half. So they are now separated by 5 meters. Again reduce the distance by half, thereby the distance between them now being 2.5 meters. If you keep doing this, the two objects will keep coming closer to each other. When will they meet? Think. The answer is: never! Yes, for all practical purposes, and for conducting some scientific experiments (depending on the degree of accuracy required), we can say that they will eventually meet. But will they, really? Even when we humans feel the two objects are in contact, if we zoom into the situation, get massive microscopes in place; we will continue to discover a huge gap between them.

How do we define *huge*?

The huge planet earth is only a dot in the galaxy that we belong to.

The mighty sun too is a dot, depending on our scale of reference.

So, most things that we perceive as absolute lose their definitiveness the moment we alter our scale of reference.

Even the two round objects in the example above, throw up a picture of well-defined objects. But, are their surfaces really well defined? Take any object, say, a table. The defined external surface is only an illusion. Science tells us that if we probe deeper and deeper into the material we will be faced with atoms and molecules, which are actually in motion, with plenty of hollow spaces in between. Concepts like electron cloud or probability of electrons being in a given position around a nucleus, all question what we see with our naked eyes and believe to be the only truth.

I say this not to question science, but to emphasize that science itself helps us to question many of our so-called objective beliefs.

In fact science is raising more and more questions.

I am all for research.

Every new insight into scientific research throws open further questions.

It has to go on like this.

Eventually science is taking us closer to spirit.

Very early in life, I had felt that physics has a lot to do with spirituality. Exactly how, I find it difficult to explain in words. Some writers have attempted to do that.

As a young boy I had the following dilemma:

I step out of my apartment.

There is no one inside.

I peep inside till the last moment before I finally shut the door.

Does everything inside the apartment *look* the same, when I am present inside as opposed to when I am not?

Does the cuckoo clock chime the same way at every half hour?

Something within me questioned whether everything remained the same when I am not in the room, even though a part of me with my scientific training was discarding this question as ridiculous! I found an answer much later that was fully compatible with science. This is how it goes.

When I am present, say in a room, I am able to watch several things around me.

What about so many *things* present in the room that I cannot see or sense?

For instance, I can see only objects that either emit or reflect light within a range of frequency that our eyes are sensitive to.

Light as we understand is nothing but a collection of electromagnetic waves of varying frequency or wavelength.

Wavelengths of electromagnetic radiation that fall between 380 nanometers (what we see as violet colour) and 750 nanometers (red colour), constitute the visible light segment, with intervening colours like indigo, blue, green, yellow and orange. Remember, VIBGYOR: the rainbow colours? Beyond this range, on either end, our eyes do not respond to electromagnetic radiations. We cannot see objects that emit or reflect rays beyond this range.

Imagine so many things we are just not able to see!

When you see the red sofa set in your room, it appears red because the light reflected off it includes waves, which are closer to the 750 nm end of the visible spectrum. The sofa is also reflecting thousands of other rays across a wide range of wavelengths, but they have no effect on our eyes. There could be zillions of rays crisscrossing the room: radio waves, television waves, or mobile telephony waves to name just a few. There are many substances that emit radiations that we cannot see, but they can harm us. Some harm us but can be of use in medical diagnosis, like X-ray. But we can see none of them.

Just like rays, there are physical waves moving around. Again, similar to electromagnetic waves, only a small range is audible to us as sound. We cannot hear anything below or above this range. Like X-ray, ultrasound waves help us in medical diagnosis, but we cannot hear ultra sound.

Then there are gases: oxygen, nitrogen, carbon dioxide, several pollutants, particulate matter, bacteria, viruses... we can see none of these. I cannot see what each visible object is made of - the atoms, molecules, electrons. I cannot see the flow of electricity either.

It does not end here. When we have a view of the room, we see only those objects that are in our line of vision. In other words, all things that are blocked by something else cannot be seen, for obvious reasons. So I cannot see objects behind the sofa set, but they are there! I only see the external walls, not the brick and mortar that make up the walls.

Imagine, if we could see all of that!

What we were getting as *a view* of the room would be completely different. It would look like anything but a room!

Yet, that is reality.

But we are so used to taking our *view* of the external world as the ultimate reality. By logical extension, what we perceive as the physical, external world, is nothing but an image created on the retina within our eyes, to which a meaning is attached by the brain. It is far from reality. The total visual sensory span that we humans enjoy, with both eyes open, is less than 180°. We are completely blind to what is behind us unless we take the help of gadgets like a rear view mirror. Now, imagine if we enjoyed 360° X-ray vision, down to the level of microbes like the virus, what kind of an external world it would have been! We would not have been functional with that kind of ability. All that I have stated above is 100 per cent compatible with science.

Yet we tend to contest and disagree whenever spiritually wise persons have stated that the external world is only an illusion created by us.

The external world is unique to each one of us, as we, as the seer, are part of the world.

We create an illusion, which we believe as the only true version of the world that we see.

You need not get obsessed with this idea.

> **ENJOY THE EXTERNAL WORLD, FROM THE VANTAGE POINT OF THE WISDOM THAT WHAT YOU SEE OR OBSERVE IS NOT THE REAL WORLD.**

A full understanding or appreciation of this aspect is not essential for your journey towards FUNDAMENTAL HAPPINESS.

Once you are on the journey, you may well be able to start appreciating these aspects of human existence.

The tiny piece of advice from me is that please do not attach too much importance to the physical world.

An appreciation of this limited aspect will help you to shed your undue attachment with the material world.

Yet, as I have said before, enjoy the external world, from the vantage point of the wisdom that what you see or observe is not the real world.

This wisdom also helps us transcend the most dreadful manifestation of the basic human condition – the fear of death.

We sometimes feel it, but are mostly able to successfully avoid it through a mix of distraction and objectivity.

My apologies, if I have sounded a little heavy on content in this section. Many books on spirituality start with a heavy dose of all this. Many of us trained to be objective with a scientific attitude could find it absurd. Yet, these are extraordinarily powerful realizations, which I wanted all readers of this book to get a flavor of. I also tried not to sound abstract, or outside this world. The need to establish the amenability to scientific thought was necessary. In any case, the external world, the way we perceive it, bereft of distractions, denials, support systems or evasions, is full of absurdity, meaninglessness, emptiness, which many internally sensitive persons are able to feel.

No one likes a Micro Manager!!

THE
SPRITUAL
CEO

11

I n an earlier section I talked about the possibility of enjoying life just below FUNDAMENTAL HAPPINESS.

At this stage in your life, you are well on the road to spirituality.

You can see both the dimensions of life clearly – the spiritual dimension full of bliss and joy, as well as the physical world.

You do not have to detest the physical world; you just need to be aware of what it represents.

By all means enjoy your glass of wine, or game of golf.

But know them for what they actually are.

Before reaching this stage, you probably attached undue importance to all of these.

As long as you are conscious and awake and recognize the true worth of all things material, you will never define yourself by them and you'll be close to FUNDAMENTAL HAPPINESS.

Remember, this one-step-below-FUNDAMENTAL HAPPINESS is also not a static position.

You are on a journey.

Every moment you are moving closer to spirit, with occasional slides. The more you recognize and cherish this journey, the more spirit will you discover in yourself.

> **YOU DO NOT HAVE TO DETEST THE PHYSICAL WORLD; YOU JUST NEED TO BE AWARE OF WHAT IT REPRESENTS.**
>
> **BY ALL MEANS ENJOY YOUR GLASS OF WINE, OR GAME OF GOLF.**
>
> **BUT KNOW THEM FOR WHAT THEY ACTUALLY ARE.**

If you have come this far reading this book, you will be able to guess what it is to be a spiritual CEO.

I am listing some insights below, based on my experience not only as a CEO but in other leadership positions as well:

1. As brought out in an earlier chapter, your worldview changes when you dwell one step below FUNDAMENTAL HAPPINESS and you begin looking at the world from a higher level. As a CEO this translates in your never missing out on the big picture. Many bright and successful leaders flounder in leadership positions essentially because they are not able to give up being micro-managers. As a spiritual CEO, you are living life at a much higher level than *normal* beings. By *higher* I am not referring to a hierarchical position or any other kind of superiority. It is not about good or bad. It is just that you have moved up life's evolutionary ladder. Because you now see things from a vantage point you automatically give up

micro-management. From this position, you can never miss the woods for the trees.

2. Your demeanor, stance, level of confidence will be of a different kind. There will be no arrogance or ego. These aspects have no place in spiritual existence. Yet you will enjoy a *power,* which will arise from within. Others will look up to you. They will see something special in you. Some will say it is your articulation skill; others will say it is due to your charisma or the like. They will not know what makes you special. In any case, that should not matter to you.

3. Your problem solving skills will get honed because instead of being overtaken by difficulties you will find space between you and the problem. This space is crucial because it enables you to approach challenges in the workplace, and face the problems in life. Earlier probably you perceived problems as extensions of your own self.

4. You will find it easy to build trust. It works both ways: you will trust others more and find it reciprocated. You will earn a level of respect that will be unprecedented. People will see you as a role model.

5. Whatever vision you paint for the team, company, or your followers will appear compelling to them. One of the essential outcomes of successful leadership is to hold a compelling vision for your team. This vision results from your deep insight and conviction. It is not borrowed from somewhere or dictated by someone that you merely transplant before your team, group or company.

6. You will never operate from an egoic position of power. It is not about abandoning the position that you have. Rather, you will notice that the hierarchy is incidental. You will use your position power judiciously. The more you use position power, the less powerful you get.

7. You will display compassion that will be seen and picked up by your followers. Yet you will be in a position to assert and clearly articulate your expectations. You will see your team members as human beings rather than *things* – mere clogs in a machine. That will not prevent you from being tough with some, but the strictness will not come from your ego.

8. Even when you have to be firm or pull up someone, the person at the receiving end will continue to respect you. You will find that you do not have to be a taskmaster. People working with you will enjoy your leadership and direction; they will try and emulate you.

9. Just like that space between you and the problems, you will find that crucial space between you, and the position you are holding. You will not let yourself get fully identified with the position.

10. As a spiritual CEO, you will create a joyful and soulful organization. Just like we humans need to connect with spirit, organizations too need to recognize the collective organizational spirit and connect with it.

11. You will never be threatened by or be jealous of an exceptionally bright subordinate, for you will be bereft of the usual human insecurities. Rather, you will be able to create an atmosphere, which brings out the best in such a subordinate, which in turn will add value to the organization.

These are not make-believe selling points. If you have read up to this point, you will be able to gauge the power behind each of the points enumerated above. You will get so empowered that, to your surprise, you will be able to do much more with less effort.

If you are able to relate to the qualities of a spiritual boss, you can also visualize the bosses and leaders who are far removed from spirit. Many of them could even be counted as *successful*.

Yet some of them may be remembered as terrible individuals. For such bosses, the only emotions that the subordinates have are fear and disdain. There is no respect for such a boss. Eventually, even the fear recedes, as the subordinates learn to cope with the diatribes and spin their own methods to escape the boss. Only contempt remains for the boss. What a pitiable existence! Now, the boss can well question: 'so what?' Indeed, how does it matter what his team is feeling about him, as long as the work gets done? Well, actually the work could probably have gotten done much better, had he not created these negative emotions. What matters is, that he has blocked creative thinking amongst his team members. Newer, greater ideas that could have come are lost. This could lead to frustration and even attrition amongst the brighter lot that he has. Finally, whom do you think the boss has been most cruel with? Many of you would have got it right. He has been most cruel with his own self, followed by his close family members, in many cases!

I'm a person of Spirit

THE
SPIRITUAL
SUBORDINATE

T he section on Spiritual CEO could have left speculation about spirituality being postponed till one reaches a leadership position. Remember, it is not only the CEO who is a leader. Many of his followers / team members are leaders themselves, for their respective teams.

So leveraging spirit to become an effective leader applies at all levels of leadership. The best part is that spirit also helps you to be a very effective subordinate. There is no ultimate authority in this world.

Everyone has a *boss*, so to say.

All CEOs have to deal with a Board and its Chairman.

Often we have to deal with very difficult bosses. If you are a Fundamentally Happy person or dwell close to FUNDAMENTAL HAPPINESS you can become an effective subordinate. You know what support you can extract from your superior. You are aware of what positive attributes of your boss's traits you could leverage, and what aspects of his personality you may safely ignore.

Effective subordinate, does not mean you find ways to please your superior, or try to gain his confidence, or become his favorite.

The idea is that you become effective in your role, improve your team's performance, be a good leader yourself, gain from the positives in your boss and not get affected by his negatives.

Apart from all other gains, you yourself are the biggest gainer.

If you are wondering how this will be possible, just go back and reflect on all benefits of living one level below FUNDAMENTAL HAPPINESS that I dwelt upon in some sections before this.

Ego is your biggest hurdle.

It comes in the way of benefitting from a good boss.

And it lets his difficult side negatively affect you.

> **THE IDEA IS THAT YOU BECOME EFFECTIVE IN YOUR ROLE, IMPROVE YOUR TEAM'S PERFORMANCE, BE A GOOD LEADER YOURSELF, GAIN FROM THE POSITIVES IN YOUR BOSS AND NOT GET AFFECTED BY HIS NEGATIVES.**

Often my ego does not permit me to appreciate the virtues of my leader, and I refuse to accept that someone could approach something better than I can. Also, very often, some externally visible *negativity* in my boss is taken very seriously, and that may hide a wealth of positives that you could build on. Once again, the ego is the culprit that does not allow us to see beyond the external irritants.

Finally, your superior could really have major personality issues. Many *bosses* are known to be intemperate, didactic, poor listeners, judgmental and, most often, very insecure. Your success and abilities may rattle some bosses. How do you deal with all of these traits? Here too, a person of spirit, by virtue of a vantage-point view of the world, is able to look differently at all of these. That does not mean that you always agree to live with a cantankerous boss. Here is a summary of how you could go about it with the help of your spirit.

1. As a person of spirit, you will know what aspects or parts of your boss's persona you will work on, and what part you will ignore. Even a difficult boss can have aspects in his persona or a certain insight that you can leverage upon and try to derive benefits for your own workspace and for your team. The rest of the *difficult* part of your boss can often be ignored or positively dealt with. The biggest advantage that any person of spirit has is to wipe out the *noise*, and look beyond. Our ego is the first to latch on to noise. Getting entangled with noise is time put to waste while generating negativity. Beyond this, you will know all the rest of the sound bites emanating from your boss that you could just ignore.

2. Your straightforwardness, focus and sincerity will take a lot of stress away from your boss. He will trust you more. This gain in trust is the hallmark of all those closer to spirit.

3. There could still be that disruptive leader, the micro manager, who will give you no space, and will tell you exactly what to do. By and large a spiritual person is able to claim his space. This happens by the way you engage with your boss. Your confidence, conviction, determination, ability to look him in

the eye and speak, without being discourteous, all can help. You must be able to do this not just with a physical stance but also with conviction.

4. Despite all of this, you may have to occasionally confront your boss. Many of us avoid confrontations and, in the process, keep suffering and sulking. Confrontation requires courage, confidence, and knowledge, but more than anything else it requires belief in self. Often a good round of confrontation backed with facts and figures helps. If your boss's style puts you through humiliation, try telling him what his style does to you. That way instead of directly criticizing him, you are only putting forward practical difficulties you face due to his inappropriate utterances. There could be valid practical concerns stemming from a humiliating style adopted by your boss. As a spiritual person, your ego might not get hurt, but for practical reasons, or for sake of good order, it may still be necessary to address it. You will be the best judge to decide what can be ignored and what needs to be confronted. I doubt whether any human being will change his style just because someone confronts him for it. But the chances are that his behavior towards you might change substantially. You may also have to remind him at intervals through an occasional, subtle hint.

5. Finally, there could be a crux situation that you just cannot function due to a disruptive boss. You may want to quit. Any decision to quit is usually a mix of emotional and practical reasons. A person close to FUNDAMENTAL HAPPINESS will take this decision mostly based on how far he will be able to perform his role, if he were to continue. If there are major roadblocks everywhere, and this comes in the way of your own leadership position, it is often better to quit rather than be a lame duck leader. Two attributes of a spiritual person

separate him from the rest in such situations. His decision will not be a reaction, and he will not keep revisiting his decision or curse his boss. He will own up his decision and move on with life. The ego will prompt you to keep complaining about this boss – about your miserable life because of him, about your decision to quit because of him, about life being better without him. All this indulgence will make no difference to your ex-boss; it will just increase your own unhappiness. One of the biggest attributes of a person of spirit is that he knows when to get off. He will know when to just leave an argument that is going nowhere. He will not prolong issues only to satisfy his ego.

You would notice that what I state for a boss-subordinate relationship applies to almost every relationship. You will find people complaining about their parents, spouses, children, in-laws and friends; almost everyone. Proximity to FUNDAMENTAL HAPPINESS helps you to move to that level in your life where you focus on what goes on within rather than deflecting attention to someone or something external. Rather you can take a considered decision and move on with life.

13

SPIRIT AND WEALTH CREATION

I have spent all my work life in the financial world. Within the context of our spiritual well-being, I have, for long, been thinking about a particular aspect of human behavior: financial investments – *how is it relevant to spiritual well-being?*

Behavioral Economics is a branch of economics that deals with the effects of social, cognitive and emotional aspects of economic decisions. Such decisions have a bearing on the market prices and resource allocation. The main focus is on the fact that we do not necessarily make economic decisions based on rational logic. It is not my intention to delve into the complexities of Behavioral Economics here. I wish to stress upon the fact that our stupidity and irrationality in matters of financial investments can be also addressed by a dose of spirit.

Here's how.

Before I begin, here are some facts about the situation on the ground.

First we have to appreciate that India is primarily a nation of savers.

As individuals we feel comfortable to put away a substantial amount of money in bank fixed deposits, where there is a certainty of the interest quantum.

That the post-tax interest earned does not beat inflation in most years is often ignored.

We avoid uncertainties and buy peace.

In an earlier section I have mentioned how, uncertainty, often a corollary to freedom, increases our angst. That is human nature. We like predictability. It keeps our fundamental unease at check.

The second major economic decision is to buy gold.

And, Indians just love the yellow metal!

There could be some merit in accumulating gold in one's life, which could be consumed in weddings or passed on to next generations.

I concede that. But much of the desire to hoard gold is an emotional reaction.

There is good reason for gold to form some part of your overall portfolio allocation.

A lot of money is getting invested in real estate too in India.

The problem arises when this allocation is not in sync with one's savings potential, risk taking ability, and the time frame one has in mind.

What lurks beneath this psychology to accumulate gold or create a lopsided portfolio is human greed. In particular, many Indians now seem to suffer from a deep desire of making it big in life, through a short cut, if possible.

This greed often causes unwise financial investments.

Creation of wealth is a good idea. It should be planned with a time frame in mind. In fact the youth of India often does not pay close attention to wealth creation at all. Creating a good, balanced portfolio that is expected to grow over a reasonably long time horizon is something all of us should do. Now where does spirit come into this?

By now you realize that I am trying to draw your attention to the fact that humans living close to FUNDAMENTAL HAPPINESS do not need external props to make their lives meaningful and happy. They are fundamentally happy – well, almost. This happiness comes because they are focused inwards, tuning in to their inner self, especially the existential suffering within, if any, and they give up a craving for external distractions and kicks in life. In fact they are pretty much content with a deeper existence.

Greed is the least likely trait that you might discover in a person close to FUNDAMENTAL HAPPINESS.

For such a person, the idea of creation of wealth is as important as any other ordinary thing in his life.

If he is in a job, he tries to be true to his role and expectations, and does what his responsibility dictates.

His job does not define him. He does enjoy the successes and the perks that come with the job.

But these do not define him or completely take him over.

He never approaches a job with the sole focus on the advantages it would bring to him.

He never operates from ego and so he never gets addicted to anything in life.

Much the same way, his investments are done with a sense of responsibility towards himself and his dependents.

If his portfolio progresses well, he undoubtedly derives satisfaction from it, but he does not cling to his portfolio.

He does not assess his portfolio every day.

He does not get tempted into short cuts of getting rich overnight.

He takes sound, professional advice if he does not himself understand the nuances of investment.

He invests through mutual funds to benefit from the expertise available with reputed fund houses. He invests through Systematic Investment Plans, and stays invested over a longer period, without being unnerved by the rise and fall of the market. He benefits from the equity growth potential by investing incrementally over a reasonably long time horizon taking proper advice wherever necessary. He understands that disciplined equity investments over a long time period help build wealth. This is not to suggest that he will not keep money in bank fixed deposits. It is a question of a balanced and disciplined approach. He does not look at equity investments as gamble where one can win or lose. Neither does he make financial portfolio management his all-time occupation.

> **GREED IS THE LEAST LIKELY TRAIT THAT YOU MIGHT DISCOVER IN A PERSON CLOSE TO FUNDAMENTAL HAPPINESS.**
>
> **FOR SUCH A PERSON, THE IDEA OF CREATION OF WEALTH IS AS IMPORTANT AS ANY OTHER ORDINARY THING IN HIS LIFE.**

The percentage of Indians who invest in the stock market, either directly or through mutual funds is very low. People do not have the time or inclination to understand the basic issues surrounding mutual funds. There is no great understanding about insurance either. I doubt how many people buy insurance products understanding what they stand for. It is a different matter that a high payout to intermediaries is helping the business grow. People are just running after instant gratification. When you are removed from spirit, you will tend to do that – look for quick pleasures.

The biggest support from a spiritual inclination comes during times when markets are not performing well. At times there can be longish periods of market indifference or a downslide. A peaceful person will not get identified with his portfolio. He will always find space between himself and his investments. A spiritual person always finds this space between him and everything else, good or bad. For the majority, a portfolio hit by the market will appear to hit him personally. Such an investor will be shaky, restless and desperate for action. On the other hand during market boom periods he will go and invest recklessly. The usual unease, anxiety, hopelessness, despair that is the characteristic of basic human existence finds its expression while dealing with financial investments as well. That is how we see repeated patterns of retail investors investing in equity markets close to the peaks and exiting near the market bottom.

A spiritual person will approach everything he does from a position of peace. You would have appreciated by now, that when you are experiencing FUNDAMENTAL HAPPINESS and receiving bouts of joy, your basic stance is that of peace. If there is one word to define a spiritual person, it is *peace*, more than *happiness*. Peace is invaluable. Peace helps you take the right decisions, and also peacefully face the consequences of any wrong decisions. It is the same, whether you are a small or a big investor, an ordinary worker, a senior executive or a CEO.

14

SPIRITUAL
RELATIONSHIPS

I have mentioned earlier that one of the traps humans fall into is to get into romantic relationships hoping to cover their inner malaise and emptiness. It is a desperate attempt at making oneself whole and complete. Humans do suffer incompleteness – remember *Aadhe Adhure*?

Popular cinema and traditional literature have further entrenched this belief that romantic love is the ultimate bliss. Yet there are works of serious literature as well as movies, which have brought out the un-sustainability of the security cover of *love* and the inevitability of partners blaming each other.

We humans do many things to stay away from our FUNDAMENTAL UNHAPPINESS. Falling in love is just one of them. It helps to get a soothing and comforting feeling of completeness. Since it is only a cover, it is bound to wear off, like so many other security blankets we tend to deploy. The reason we suffer has to do with our spirits, and no amount of protection of the external world will give us lasting peace. In such relationships, each partner is actually using the other to fill the void within.

Love is always for my sake. It attempts to satisfy my need.

Even going by the classical theory of motivation propounded by Maslow, we humans are driven by a hierarchy of needs. The need for belongingness and love is a somewhat higher level need compared to the basic ones like food, shelter and security. But we can get horribly stuck at this level of *need to be loved*, instead of moving up to *need for self-esteem and self-actualization*. In fact many decisions of our life stem from our low self-esteem. Psychologists define self-esteem as a person's overall emotional evaluation of his or her own worth. We feel worthless and try out things, which give us a sense of self, approval or even attention. Just like a child can get disruptive, even violent to seek attention, we adults often do similar things out of our low self-esteem. A critical close look might reveal the same human condition lurking beneath the low self-esteem. Your upbringing and circumstances could also be a reason for your low self-esteem. It is easy to blame our circumstances for what we are today but if we take courage and authentically face ourselves as responsible for our present state, we might notice that at the core of our low self-esteem lurks FUNDAMENTAL UNHAPPINESS.

Under such circumstances, how long can a fairy tale romantic love last?

We can only fool ourselves.

I have been cautioning all along, and would again hasten to add that I have absolutely no moral problems with falling in love, celebrating Valentine's Day, young couples having a nice private moment in a park, or couples breaking away from a bad or abusive relationship. I am all for that freedom. The so-called moral police or *khap panchyats* have no place in a modern world. Rather, the more you have fallen in and out of love, the more you are likely to question it someday and move beyond.

Falling in love can be a very good start, provided you move up and beyond *romantic love* and view the relationship from a different perspective. As your relationship matures, you move on from the lovey-dovey part to one of mutual respect, understanding, sharing, trust, and caring. You become partners in life. All love marriages that are still lasting would have transcended beyond romantic love to these matured aspects of life and have thereby re-invented and broadened the very meaning of *romance*. Among the celebrities, I can see many in this category, but would not like to name them to maintain good order.

Getting to know your partner is like any journey with ups and downs. Every joyful relationship would have had its share of struggle and pain. As we get rid of these stumbling blocks, we learn to keep our egos at bay, and move on to a higher plane within the relationship.

Some would, perhaps, visualize such mature relationships as boring and mundane. People closer to FUNDAMENTAL HAPPINESS will be able to appreciate that these non-clinging, mature relationships of mutual space add a lot of spark and joy to life. Life, in any case, is mostly joyful for persons who dwell just below FUNDAMENTAL HAPPINESS.

> **THE IRONY IS THAT PARTNERS CAN LIVE THE BEST LIVES WHEN THEY REALLY DON'T *NEED* EACH OTHER. YOU CAN TRULY LOVE A PERSON WITHOUT *NEEDING* HIM OR HER. THIS *NEED* IS THE SOURCE OF A LOT OF MISERY.**

If you notice, the fights, which happen between *loving* couples mostly arise from the mind-ego combination.

'You did not pay attention to me',

'You did not care for me',

'You are not like before' are some of the usual complaints.

Both partners keep looking for the initial spark. There is lack of trust. They blame each other. Obviously here each partner operates from his or her inner needs, which are not getting satisfied anymore.

Even while you are somehow managing a turbulent relationship and facing occasional abuse, you may still find it impossible to think of calling quits or staying alone. You have actually made your partner your *emotional crutch*. Despite a troubled relationship, your partner is, nevertheless, *completing* you. You cannot let go. You *need* your partner badly. This *need* arises out of your inner condition, which you are in denial of. Chances are you will finally lose your partner when he or she finally decides to dump you. Or you will walk out on your own only after you have lined up another partner. The trick lies in facing the peril of the possibility of having to live without your partner. However, at this point an actual break up may not be necessary. But the mere thought of estrangement may make you feel empty. Stay with the emptiness. Feel the pain for a few days. You could gradually start feeling better. Now you are on your journey. You don't *need* your partner any more. There will be no *need* to complete yourself through a partner. Yet, your relationship with him or her may actually improve radically. You will find peace. The irony is that partners can live the best lives when they really don't *need* each other. You can truly love a person without *needing* him or her. This *need* is the source of a lot of misery.

Yet, you will be able to complement each other much better than before.

What is true for couples is also true for almost any other relationship: parent and child, siblings, colleagues, or neighbors. Problems arise when we try to derive a sense of self from these relationships. This is most often the case when parents look to fulfilling their own aspirations through their children and push them into making choices, which according to their view are appropriate. Why can't parents just allow their children to be? By all means we, as parents, should try to give our children the best education and impart good values. Value system is best imparted by walking the talk. The child observes the modeling parent and makes a judgment about the value system. There is no point lecturing. The best upbringing a parent can give to the child is to be available for all discussions, exchange of all ideas, without any barrier. Such discussions are best held at *equal* footing rather than the parent taking a superior role. You need a lot of peace, confidence and a high degree of trust to make this happen. A spiritual person close to FUNDAMENTAL HAPPINESS will be ready for this. He or she would probably also awaken the spirit in the children.

15.

THE
SPIRITUAL
YOUTH

It should be apparent to all readers of this book that the foundation of FUNDAMENTAL HAPPINESS is peace and not *happiness* in the way we understand the word. We look for happiness mostly as a way of keeping our FUNDAMENTAL UNHAPPINESS in check or under wraps. The core of FUNDAMENTAL HAPPINESS is peace – lasting, durable peace. Once you taste this peace within, you are fundamentally happy - in a state of bliss.

It may not show externally. It is not the kind of excited happiness derived out of some external stimulus that could temporarily reflect on all aspects of your personality, until it wears out.

Your FUNDAMENTAL HAPPINESS is your own, and those surrounding you or close to you may not get to know anything about it.

What they might notice is your being special, positively different from the rest, peaceful, insightful, compassionate, understanding, yet principled, courageous and forthright.

Peace is that invaluable gift that we can get if we find our way to

111

FUNDAMENTAL HAPPINESS or come close to it.

Peace may throw up different meanings to different people.

People past mid age might be in a position to sense how valuable peace is.

The young might not readily agree.

Some youngsters may think peace to be a kind of speed breaker in the zest for life.

How many of you living your lives at enormous speed, are ready to take a pause?

Are you ready to look at yourselves square in the face?

Are you open that you might discover newer dimensions of life?

> **THE CORE OF FUNDAMENTAL HAPPINESS IS PEACE — LASTING, DURABLE PEACE. ONCE YOU TASTE THIS PEACE WITHIN, YOU ARE FUNDAMENTALLY HAPPY - IN A STATE OF BLISS.**

My own struggles with FUNDAMENTAL UNHAPPINESS, and the eventual embarkation on a journey towards FUNDAMENTAL HAPPINESS, have straddled my youth, middle age as well as the senior stage of my life. It took me a long time for I was not on the correct path for years. I kept trying what now in retrospect was a foolish struggle – struggle against the suffering, trying to distract, avoiding and hoping to become *normal* again, until I had courage to look inwards and go beyond my suffering. That said I do not regret this delay. The time was very well spent. More than anything else I have had the advantage of seeing things differently during my youth. I have to concede that the life led by the youth then was possibly slower than today. There were fewer night clubs. Internet, and all that goes with it, were completely absent.

We indulged in actual, physical games like cricket or football. Music was limited to the radio (no FM, only AM!). It would still be worthwhile to share some of my thoughts on what a life of spirit could mean for the youth.

If you rewind and go back a few chapters, you will remember that the need for fulfillment is a basic human requirement. All of us want fulfillment, though we end up doing the wrong things. This universal paradigm holds true for youth too.

When I see, in particular, the Indian youth today, I notice passion, energy, alacrity, courage, expression, questioning, independence and aspiration. The sum total of all these emotions makes a complete human. What I also see in the youth is impatience, restlessness, anger, and a sense of despair about the direction of their lives; they are often emotionally on the edge. They are also able to pick up new things in life without help – e-mode, internet, or discovering the social media. I know that there are some countries or geographies where the youth may be suppressed and unable to think aloud or express themselves on crucial issues concerning them or society. Where they are free, I am actually happy to see the cauldron of the entire spectrum of emotions in today's youth. I think we were much more constrained when I was young. But the times were different. We were compelled to be normative. There was, in those times, acute information or knowledge arbitrage. Today, information and awareness travel at the speed of light. I would have been worried and disappointed had today's youth been mechanical, suppressed, or just conforming to given standards of behavior. In a sense today's youth experiences more freedom.

If you recall, I had mentioned in an earlier section that with freedom comes more anxiety, dread, tentativeness and despair. It would be a fair assessment if I averred that today's youth lives a life with the basic human condition or the FUNDAMENTAL

UNHAPPINESS just under their skin. That is actually wonderful news. That gives them potential to acknowledge their current state of being and transcend it into a more insightful existence, where they can find more peace and joy at the fundamental level, yet continue to question things that, they feel, are not right, thereby making their own choices. All they need is to develop some degree of awareness within them. They need to get onto the journey enunciated in this book, take stock of themselves, understand and acknowledge themselves more authentically and move further on in life.

If they do this they will enjoy all the attributes of spiritual life. They will exercise more choices in life without getting trapped in social norms. They will be able to think out of the box, be compassionate, feel the pain of the socially disadvantaged, be more gender sensitive, be good listeners, with many of them becoming natural leaders. This does not prevent them from having fun. Instead, as I always maintain, having fun will have a much more relaxed tone, without any of the attendant desperation which is often noticed now. Their relationships could move to a more mature level, several notches above the fairy tale romantic love that some might be experiencing now. Such relationships will be more of the non-clinging type, based on mutual space and respect. There will not be any pressure on either partner to keep the other *entertained*. If one partner feels like watching a movie, and the other one feels like taking a nap, it will not lead to a catastrophe. Each partner will understand.

The youth will have to understand the murky designs of the ego. This is true of all humankind – anyone who wants to enjoy the fruits of FUNDAMENTAL HAPPINESS and spiritual life. I believe ego is less pronounced in most of youth as compared to those who are in their middle ages or beyond. Successful seniors are likely to be the biggest prisoners of their egos. I also believe that if they are convinced, the youth will easily connect with their inner condition. Anything that the youth is convinced of, they will pursue without hesitation or affirmations from others.

I have great hopes in the youth who can transform our country and contribute to the transformation of the world. They will find it easier to move towards more authenticity. They have to ponder, take stock of themselves and then take the plunge. You can still enjoy the good things in life, have a party, and enjoy your drink. There will be a shift in the quality of your enjoyment.

16

BRAND
LOYALTY

Developing and retaining brands occupies a substantial amount of mind space of business leaders. It is necessary to promote and preserve brand names, to continue business. Where some brands do not work, attempts are made at rebranding exercises to salvage them. Brands are also valued, whereby an amount is attached to it as its financially embedded value. This value often determines the consideration for mergers and acquisitions. It is no matter of any doubt that brand is very important.

There are brands that are built around trust, reliability, and quality of service or product outreach. Whenever you talk *brand* you have a market in mind. There could be strong brands well entrenched in rural areas or smaller cities. Similarly there are brands that appeal to the elite.

There are brands that are backed by tangible deliverables. *Value for money* is a very real and practical way of getting attached to a brand. There are numerous examples amongst airlines, banks,

FMCG companies, hoteliers, card companies, fund houses, hospitals, colleges, universities that deliver what we perceive as value for money. There is satisfaction with their engagement and there is strong recall value.

There is another kind of brand, which is purely backed by emotions, need for showing off, urge to keep up with the Joneses, or fundamentally to give the self a sense of thrill or reassurance amidst a confused and tentative existence. We cling to these brands for dear life, as if they are part of us. Like many other props we build to keep ourselves afloat in a fundamentally unhappy situation, we need to question whether we are doing something similar with brands. Well-known brand owners would hate me for this, but I am bewildered at what people can spend on intangibles. The entire advertising space, brand-positioning industry, along with the culture of consumerism, play on the minds of hapless people who, at a fundamental level, are at a loss to derive a meaning out of their senseless existence. Eventually, they latch on to a brand for giving them that meaning or conformity. An external prop obviously lasts only for a while, so soon enough people start to search for more or other new ones. The manufacturers and advertisers also keep their supply lines of more exotic products alive.

Please do not mistake me. I am not coming from any moral position at all. I am against any kind of a suggested ban on consumerism, or celebrating Valentine's Day. Nothing should be banned. I stand by and respect a free society. All I wish to underline here is the need to question what prompts us to blindly desire unreasonable number of things in the external world. All those who have a spiritual quest and have embarked on an inward journey, certainly need to ponder over this. I have no problems with those who are fine with the way they are. I also do not support the leftist view against consumerism.

Actually I am a little wary of all *'ists'*, including left*ists*, right*ists*, acti*vists*, and environmenta*lists*. Many social activists have made valuable contributions to mankind. The problem arises, when some activists completely identify with their *cause* and close their eyes to everything else. Somewhere their ego has come into play, which brings in the *self* as the central feature of their work. Mahatma Gandhi, Martin Luther King and Nelson Mandela, to take a few names, have made immense contribution to mankind. They operated through a value system and painted a vision for the future, which was so compelling that people followed them. The ones, who opposed, had to give up. But none of them were activists. They never operated from an ego position; rather it was always a principled stand. Some of the most renowned environmentalists are from the western world of developed nations, which have done maximum harm to the environment, and are today lecturing the developing world. We, developing nations, too need to be conscious of what we are doing to our planet earth through pollution of all kinds; but we need to attain a certain level of development too. However that is a separate argument.

Why do we attach so much importance to intangibles or snob value ??

Coming back to brand loyalty, from the perspective of a spiritual

journey, we need to question:

What value does attachment bring to our life?

What is it that gets driven by our inner urge to prop our self?

In practical day-to-day living, we need to acquire many things. This is necessary.

> **WE ARE FUNDAMENTALLY INCOMPLETE AND LOOK FOR PROPS AND DIVERSIONS.**

If you need to buy an air conditioner, by all means buy the best that you can afford. Obviously a cost-benefit analysis and some research into the various brands available help make a better choice. The problem, purely from a spiritual perspective in our journey towards FUNDAMENTAL HAPPINESS, arises when we attach too much importance to intangibles, or to snob value.

Scratch yourself; you might notice your ego playing a major role.

Brand consciousness sometimes reaches laughable proportions. I am aghast when I find teenagers, school goers harp and brag about brands. I once bought a Digital SLR Camera to cater to my interests in photography. This replaced an earlier version of SLR camera that I owned dating back to the film roll era. I obviously did some survey to know about the various features that different makes had to offer. Since all manufacturers are based outside India, I was keen to know the kind of customer support available domestically. To be honest, I found that most of the well-known brands offer almost the same stuff. The price range was also pretty narrow. I made a choice of a particular brand based on my happy experience with the previous film roll camera. Within the brand, I looked for the model that would suit my budget and also offer facilities and options for a bit of special photography.

When you come to sophistication, there is no stopping. You can go for higher models, with the price multiplying. The key question is: what features you are looking for, and how much of those you actually need and are going to use. Based on all these considerations I made a choice. I must concede that very often, in such matters, I am fairly impulsive. I finally go by the *gut feel*.

One teenager amongst our family friends, a very brand conscious smart young man, came to know and wanted to see the camera. I happily showed it to him. He knew, almost by rote, the model numbers of this make, prices, as well as most models being offered by competing makes. His first reaction was: *"Oh no! You should have gone for the next higher make. It would have been just 10,000 bucks more."* I tried explaining that the enhanced features would have been of little use to me. I also asserted my cost benefit analysis. I did not want to spend more. He was not impressed. Knowing how smart and aware he is, I tried to give him some tips about photography and what features to look for in a camera. I was disappointed when I realized that he was not interested in the nuances of photography, even the basics! I thought such knowledge would be interesting for him. But he quickly got out of this discussion. Yet, he knew all about the brands and the prices. This is the dilemma. We feel compelled to *own* stuff that gives us a *feel good* effect, helps us feel proud, adequate or complete, even though the thing we own may not serve any true value to us.

In many countries there is a flourishing industry for producing fake branded-like stuff. People who buy them also know that they are spurious items being sold as *look-alikes*. It is so important to own these brands and flaunt them! Honestly, I feel sad for them. We find ourselves amidst a very tentative existence. We are fundamentally incomplete and look for props and diversions.

Many of the brands, supported by an advertising strategy that appeals to our senses, often with hilarious claims, offer us that crucial support system to help us derive a sense of self through acquiring such brands. We feel comforted for some time, until we discover *better* and more expensive props.

17.

EGO

I t would be getting clearer by now that the biggest hurdle in our path towards a life of fulfillment is our ego. As Tolle correctly mentions, there is too much resistance in us. *"Non-resistance to what is"* is the answer. This resistance comes from our ego. A close collaborator of our ego is our mind.

You will recall my premise, stated several times in this book, that depression, anxiety, despair, sense of void – all these are often lumped together as psychiatric disorder. Treatment usually includes medication or counseling or both. Each of these treatments acts on the mind. Medication attempts to change the brain chemistry, thereby bringing in cheer, or by numbing our mental sensations so that we do not feel much. Counseling attempts to retrain the mind offering it a possibility to view the world or the problems differently. So in either case we are stuck at trying to get better at the level of mind, whereas the solution lies in working at the level of spirit. If we visualize our existence as a sum total of body, mind and spirit, there should be no difficulty in appreciating the role of spirit. This is not the occult. It is very real. If you have come this far in this book, you would have found numerous examples of manifestation of spirit.

I can recall clearly when I was suffering intensely from depression and anxiety I would occasionally just pause and take a close look at myself – my being. I was surprised to discover that there was nothing fundamentally wrong with me. Yet there was this painful condition, which I could not explain. I was fundamentally unhappy. I have to be honest that whenever I could dare to take a hard look at my state, there were occasionally, very brief spells of clarity and peace – as if there was nothing wrong. At times I have wondered whether this suffering of mine was just an illusion. I often used to wish that there would be just a simple trick and I would realize that the release from this suffering was just a step away. It was, as if I could open a door from a dark room and just step into another world. I had still not had any exposure to the spiritual writings of the modern world. So I continued to suffer. Yet, when the solution came it was not very different from what I had imagined or wished for. It was like walking through a swivel door!

My problem was neither in my body, nor mind.

My suffering was at the level of spirit.

So could targeting the mind be a solution?

One advantage of suffering for so many years was that my ego had received a severe beating. My guess is that even if I had been exposed to new age spiritual writings earlier on, my obstinate ego would probably have been an obstacle. I now realize that my years in suffering have probably made me a far more perceptive person open-minded to newer dimensions of life. I was already sick of the familiar, known dimension of life. I guess the laws of nature are like that. When you suffer, your ego succumbs and is humbled, preparing you for a new journey. It is not surprising that most spiritual writers have mentioned about suffering and the sense of release thereafter. As I have stated earlier, almost all religious texts too focus on the way out of this suffering. Literature, music, art is replete with touching descriptions of this suffering. The depictions show the sensitivity and nuances of the human suffering without a way out, possibly to preserve the beauty and depth of this state of humanness.

In the section where I have detailed the steps to be followed in the journey towards FUNDAMENTAL HAPPINESS I have suggested that it is necessary to deal with your ego. A close and honest look at oneself while on this journey would reveal that our mind and ego are the two biggest obstacles to our progression towards FUNDAMENTAL HAPPINESS.

Our egos can be pretty stubborn.

They develop repetitive patterns.

Hence dealing with ego can take time.

Simple practices can help us in this.

Answer these questions honestly:

While in conversation:

>   *Do I talk the most?*
>
>   *Am I a keen listener?*
>
>   *Do I have an open mind?*
>
>   *Am I open to learn new things, new ideas?*
>
>   *Or, do I find it difficult to accept that there are things I do not know?*
>
>   *Do I find it difficult to learn from people younger or junior to me?*
>
>   *Am I judgmental?*
>
>   *Do I have prejudices like gender bias?*

Men who can honestly face their stance on the issue of gender bias can get a good measure of their egocentricity.

I bring up all these issues, because, without our realization, they can collectively be a barrier to joyful existence. These are not complicated or challenging concepts. They are fairly simple, everyday issues, though deeply rooted and entrenched in us, and hence, difficult to shed. But you cannot expect to land anywhere near FUNDAMENTAL HAPPINESS, without shedding all these rigidities.

You can easily identify a person who operates from a strong ego. Such persons could be intrusive, overbearing, closed to fresh ideas, judgmental, impatient, insolent, aggressive, or a combination of all these. Often such people can be fairly knowledgeable and efficient too, capable of taking their organizations or teams to new successful heights. However, such success may not always be sustainable and could come at a price not immediately measurable. Most often the price comes in the form of a de-motivated human resource, leading to inefficiencies and attrition. The full potential of the team or organization, that might have witnessed success, may not have been realized.

Conversely, people who do not operate mostly from ego are also similarly identifiable. They could be humble, eager to learn, good listeners, patient, and practical. It does not automatically follow that such persons will be good leaders. That is a separate debate. The section on The Spiritual CEO dwells on some attributes you are likely to witness in a leader who lives life close to FUNDAMENTAL HAPPINESS.

Purely from the standpoint of your spiritual journey, you need to acknowledge the existence of your ego. By observing other people who could be at different positions on this scale of ego, one can question himself and also learn a few things. If you continue to operate from ego, it will emerge as a major stumbling block in your journey towards a joyful life.

Understand that it will take time. So, don't give up. Recognize and be conscious of actions that have been prompted by your ego.

Don't fight with your ego.

Just notice how it prompts you.

Remember the pattern.

Next time in a similar situation you may suddenly question your stance. Every time you question, you move up the ladder. That will help in your pursuit of a happy life.

Some may be wondering why the human experience at the basic level is that of unease, void, anxiety and melancholy. FUNDAMENTAL HAPPINESS too is a basic condition but needs to be uncovered. Why is it that we need to go beyond layers of suffering, before we can taste the FUNDAMENTAL HAPPINESS that truly belongs to us? Why has nature been so cruel to mankind? If you recall, I have devoted entirely to this aspect an earlier section titled, Why is Fundamental Human Existence So Unhappy?

I suspect that we humans suffer so much because of the way we have been using our mind and ego over centuries. We are way too intelligent compared to the closest animal species just below us on the evolutionary ladder. We have emotions. Also, we can think extremely fast, we can dream, paint a very realistic picture of the future, hatch a plot, scheme, and strategize. These are valuable tools available to mankind. Unfortunately, these tools have taken over us humans completely. The great capacity of human intellect, which has exhibited itself through discoveries, inventions, innovations over thousands of years, has also led us to completely lose touch with our selves. We have used the same mental capacity to inflict unimaginable cruelty on our own selves. I often shudder to think that over the centuries, the maximum suffering caused to human beings has been by fellow human beings, and not from natural disasters or diseases. Tolle calls this *"the collective manifestations of the insanity that lies at the heart of the human condition"*. He rightly says we have become too mind identified. His prescription is to stay in the *"present moment"*. I wholeheartedly agree with him. Being present is nothing but the surrender that all writers speak of. I have dwelt upon the same surrender in my step-by-step approach towards FUNDAMENTAL HAPPINESS. Being present is being in touch with your *Self*. Thanks to our mind and its computer like capacity we have lost this touch. And, mind and ego are close collaborators. They help and support each other.

> IF YOU FIGHT YOUR EGO, YOU ARE TRAPPED BY IT AGAIN. MY OWN EXPERIENCE SUGGESTS THAT NOTICING, DETECTING OR RECOGNIZING YOUR EGO IS IN ITSELF A VERY POWERFUL SPIRITUAL TOOL.

A direct outcome of this mind-ego dominated existence is that we lead completely unaware lives. We are actually unconscious. Through a spiritual awakening process, we increase our awareness; we actually wake up, we become conscious. By extension, all of you who feel depressed, anxious, tentative, and forlorn for no apparent reason, please remember, you feel so for you know more than the other *normal* beings, whom Tolle calls *"unconscious"*. You are more aware. The way out is not to reduce your awareness, but to grow it further to feel the FUNDAMENTAL HAPPINESS, which too is embedded deep within.

Tolle has a good prescription to make for dealing with our ego:

> *"Resentment is the emotion that goes with complaining and the mental labeling of people and adds even more energy to the ego. Resentment means to feel bitter, indignant, aggrieved, or offended. You resent other people's greed, their dishonesty, their lack of integrity, what they are doing, what they did in the past, what they said, what they failed to do,*

what they should or shouldn't have done. The ego loves it. Instead of overlooking unconsciousness in others, you make it into their identity. Who is doing that? The unconsciousness in you, the ego. ... And what you react to in another, you strengthen in yourself."

However, Tolle also cautions that *"complaining is not to be confused with informing someone of a mistake or a deficiency so that it can be put right. And to refrain from complaining doesn't necessarily mean putting up with bad quality or behavior."*

I fully agree that we must have the right to protest against corruption, gender bias or any social ill. A rapist needs to be swiftly booked and duly punished. There can also be a tightening of the sentence and stiffening of laws for crimes against women. The only important question to ask is: *'Am I being prompted by my ego?'* Ego creeps in very smartly. We may continue to fool ourselves into believing that we are only doing the right thing. One big test is to question ourselves whether we have started hating the criminal. Similarly, we need to be guarded against the adversary or a hostile nation – may be take preemptive action. But do not hate them.

Hatred is the vocabulary of the ego.

Tolle also says: *"Don't take the ego too seriously. When you detect egoic behavior in yourself, smile. At times you may even laugh. ... If you consider the ego to be a personal problem, that's just more ego."*

I repeat, if you fight your ego, you are trapped by it again. My own experience suggests that noticing, detecting or recognizing your ego is in itself a very powerful spiritual tool.

Do not punish yourself. Just observe and be aware.

18

SPIRIT AND VALUE SYSTEM

A s you stabilize in your journey and move towards FUNDAMENTAL HAPPINESS,

As you feel more connected with your *Self* and also with other beings,

As you feel that *oneness* with what surrounds you,

You are bound to discover the inherent basic goodness in you.

Probably the name *God* has come about from this goodness that we experience when we are on this journey. After all, as I have stated earlier, all religious texts also aim to show you the path to go beyond the pain of mundane human existence and transcend to a life of bliss. What I call FUNDAMENTAL HAPPINESS, or what spiritual writers have called salvation, redemption or awakening, or what existentialists like James Park call *"existential freedom"* are all different names given to that elevated level of existence where you experience peace and joy and witness the world differently. From this vantage position, negative sentiments like revenge, jealousy, insecurity, adamancy, greed, obsessive competitiveness, nurturing of old grudges, or unfair blaming disappear from your life. What you see in yourself is quite the opposite: compassion, generosity, patience, humility, courage and peaceful but well considered determination. This fundamental change in the way we see the world around us, as detailed by me in various sections of this book, also impacts the way we deal with our subordinates, superiors, family members, or society at large. The sum total of all this gets captured in our value system.

All of us imbibe a value system, which is the aggregate of the way we are brought up, the education we are exposed to, as well as our life experiences. Our value system prompts us to conduct ourselves in a particular way as we move on in life. We hear a lot of talk about general erosion in value systems, as we witness new lows in public life, corporate governance, or personal conduct. Education can help up to a point. The problem arises when we witness pressures of competiveness and the compulsion to win right from our school days, very often exacerbated by ambitious parents. So the values that could have been imbibed by a child get lost in a complex and cruel world.

It should be apparent that a dose of spirit could help us with clarifying our values. The biggest difference in your stance, closer to FUNDAMENTAL HAPPINESS, arises from the fact that you do not operate from an ego position now. Devoid of ego, you look at almost everything with a different perspective and this gets captured in your value system. It is not as if you necessarily *learn* about new values or that you *put in place* a new value system. Rather, your values get clarified and re-evaluated. These values were probably there, but were lost or buried. You are in a position to take a principled stand, for example to be able to firmly say *no* to corruption or gender bias or any other social ill. You will find new courage to be able to take such a stand. The opposite of this is a world far removed from spirit where one can see compromises at various levels prompted by lack of courage, convenience, short cuts in life or plain greed. One can see the huge positive for society at large by imparting some spirit into our lives. This is not to suggest that the vast majority of humans, who are not really on a spiritual journey, necessarily lack the values that form the foundation of a good society. We often see society take up good causes or fight against injustice. The goodness buried deep inside does get aroused. It gets reflected in many affirmative actions taken by civil society. We rise, protest, may be even scream. Then we are back to our *normal* lives. Individually most of us are sick of the lows that society has collectively reached.

Even different values can form the foundation of a good society

There is need for raising the bar at the society level. Education, lecturing or training could play a limited role. Eventually the lasting effect is to be found through spirit. This value system has to become part of the DNA of human society at large.

Interestingly, you will notice that most people who take up social causes often display a fair degree of angst. You may notice many of them as *troubled* when they lecture or while they are on TV shows. That is natural for they are basically sensitive individuals. They feel their inner condition more than others. That way they are on the brink of a movement towards FUNDAMENTAL HAPPINESS. In contrast, those who are leading fully contended lives are least likely to take up a social cause and invest time and energy in it. It is the *disturbed, unhappy* kind who is likely to question things in life. Rather, not getting good answers to their many questions about life, and the consequent unhappiness, is itself a sign of spiritual growth. Such people are making invaluable contribution to society. Many of them could be unaware of their spirit-readiness. If they could impart some consciousness to their inner unhappiness, they could discover peace, and yet remain determined in the pursuit of their mission. A word of caution: any strong attachment with any cause, mission or campaign has the potential of taking us away from spirit. It is the same old culprit: our ego! It comes into play stealthily. If we are honest with ourselves, we can discover that at least a part of the reason for our missionary zeal could be ego. That this activity gives me *meaning* in life, and I derive a sense of self through it, could be another contributor to the passion for whatever cause we may pursue. By bringing in spirit into their lives, activists too can find that space between themselves and their mission, much like I have recommended for CEOs and other leaders to create a similar space. Do not completely identify with your work. If you create that essential space, you will be able to contribute more than before. Yet, I am not suggesting that activists must necessarily take a pause to take stock of themselves. Where a person would like to be on the spiritual scale is a personal choice.

While talking about values, I must place on record my total rejection of moral policing and many social pressures in the name of *culture*. Women face the brunt of such regressive thoughts, much more than men, though men too considerably suffer. The expectation that women should be confined to domestic chores or should dress appropriately has often been expressed by sections of the political class. In the name of values, a lot of pain is inflicted upon people just because they are having a quiet moment in a public park with a partner, or because they have a different sexual orientation.

Freedom of choice in personal life is non-negotiable.

No one can take it away from an individual.

This also extends to all those who, after reading this book, decide to reject it and continue with their lives like before. Moreover, there is nothing like a standard set of good values.

Values can differ.

We can have two individuals with different sets of values, both exemplars for a good society.

19

CONSEQUENCES OF NOT MOVING TOWARDS FUNDAMENTAL HAPPINESS

After reading most parts of this book, there could still be many who wonder: why get into all this? They may feel they are fine and happy with life. Some may even feel they are currently best positioned in their lives; that it could not be better.

Well, as I have hastened to clarify at various places, it is entirely your choice. What you do with your life is entirely up to you. My proposal is not a must-do. However, knowledge helps, especially when it has got to do with deeper aspects of our existence. Different people can be at different stages of evolution of their consciousness. Some of us are not yet ready. Some are ready but they do not realize it. They are unaware.

I am not suggesting that people who have noticed their FUNDAMENTAL UNHAPPPINESS are superior. Nor am I hinting here at any inferiority for persons who are actually suffering,

133

are mostly on the edge, on a short fuse but are blaming their circumstances or others for their predicament. They are *"unconscious"*, to borrow a phrase from Tolle. Similarly, there is no suggestion that I am pointing at any inferiority for people who are happy, without complaints about anything. To repeat what I have stated before, such people could be just plain lucky having been able to fully divert away from within themselves. They could be leading superficial lives. Their lives could be well structured with everything pre-determined and pre planned – perfect to the t. Most likely there would be no room for any subjectivity in such cases. That life could be devoid of richness is a different matter. If you are enjoying this state, please do so, as long as it lasts. There is absolutely no problem with that. It is not the bounden duty of all humans to first discover FUNDAMENTAL UNHAPPINESS and then move to FUNDAMENTAL HAPPINESS. Why take the trouble?

Based on the above I can broadly visualize three kinds of human existence:

1. Those who are happy, content and have nothing to complain about.

2. Those who are *troubled*, not-at-peace with themselves, on the edge; yet either

   (a) They are in denial and insist they are fine, or

   (b) They have a ready list of reasons for their unhappiness; ascribing it often to other people they are dealing with or to the circumstances surrounding them.

3. Those who are suffering from depression, anxiety, despair, and meaninglessness. They do not associate it with anyone or anything. They are probably doing their rounds with psychiatrists.

By now, I think, we know which category of people will benefit most from this book. Obviously, persons in category 3 are ready to take the plunge. They are like those who have seen others swimming, and have to muster courage to enter the pool and just let go. They could be happily swimming in weeks to come. However, they should take professional help whenever in doubt. I am only referring to simple depression or anxiety without any cause. Mental disorders like schizophrenia or OCD would require treatment. I am not aware whether imparting spirit to your life helps in such cases.

Persons in category 1 can wait. They seem to be fine. They can store the thoughts brought out in this book in their mind. If ever they are confronted with a situation where they have to ponder about some deeper, more fundamental aspects of life, they can go back to this book. They might feel interested then. Yet, imparting spirit in their life can bring a lot of richness and depth in an otherwise bland existence. They can begin by observing whatever unhappiness they encounter even if it is circumstantial .

I have to devote a larger part of this section towards persons in category 2. I see the world full of such persons, who need to be guided. Within that category, subsection 2 (a) could, again, take some time to prepare. They are suffering but do not as yet acknowledge it. They are in denial and such evasion seems to work. Some of them might get a jolt after reading this book. For some, the brickwork of denial will have to be strengthened. That may work too – for some time. Or, some may start wondering about themselves. My request to such people is: please take your time. Treat yourself as human. You are not a machine that turning on a switch can start a new process.

Ask as many questions as possible.

Open any page of this book and read it again.

Read it slowly.

Do not race through it.

Observe yourself as you go along. Please do not set any target time for yourself. Prepare yourself for a long journey, for the cloak of denial is very strong. It is built by the mind-ego combination. And, we humans are very smart. We are extraordinarily intelligent. So allow yourself time and treat yourself gently. At any stage you are free to reject the proposition completely and go back to your usual life. Your journey may witness a few U-turns. Never mind.

> **THOSE WHO ARE SUFFERING, AND ARE ABLE TO ACKNOWLEDGE IT, HAVE BOTH THE MOTIVATION AND THE OPPORTUNITY TO TAKE THE PLUNGE.**

My biggest concern is with all of you who consider yourselves in category 2 (b). You all are suffering. What is worse, you are probably causing a lot of suffering to others as well, and justifying it to yourself. This springs from your need to blame others or external circumstances for your current state of being. Part of your condition could well be caused by the situation you are in. Earlier on I had tried to distinguish between the circumstantial unhappiness and FUNDAMENTAL UNHAPPINESS. If you allow yourself to just observe your suffering without any resistance, without analyzing the causes for your depression or anxiety, it could be a very good starting point. It may look difficult to begin with. I invite you to follow the step-by-step approach given by me. As you progress through the steps, at some stage you will be able to simply focus on your pain without going to the reason for that pain. You might gradually notice that the pain is fundamentally within you, and that you had probably indulged in some exaggeration in ascribing your suffering to the external world. You may well reach the stage of forgiving those who you earlier blamed for your predicament. You are now on course in your journey towards spiritual bliss. You need two attributes to be able to make a beginning – truthfulness about yourself and some courage – courage of the *swimming pool* type, where you succumb to the water and float instead of fighting to float on it.

I have to add here that the categories 1, 2 (a), (b) and 3 built by me are only to help understand where we stand. They are not silos. It is a continuum. A person in one category can also find in him traces from other categories. They overlap.

We must also understand the consequences of not setting out on to this journey towards FUNDAMENTAL HAPPINESS. Those who are suffering, and are able to acknowledge it, have both the motivation and the opportunity to take the plunge.

You actually rise up by taking the dive under. You discover the joy of imparting more spirit to your life. By postponing this shift, you continue to suffer. Worse, you may suffer the physiological effects of continued stress – increased heart rate, blood pressure, loss of appetite, or the opposite – binge eating, indigestion, disturbed sleep, reduced sexual appetite etc. Stress is the source of disease of most lifestyles today.

Those who find themselves in either parts of category 2, may have added problems if they do not move up the spiritual path. Apart from continuing to suffer, they will certainly inflict a lot of pain on others. Of course they will justify it. But their lives as well as the lives of their close ones could be rather painful. When we look around we are able to identify many *difficult* people. You find them in offices, homes, parliament, and society, almost anywhere. Try to find out honestly whether you too are seen by many as a difficult person. You have to be open and get some honest feedback to be able to reach that conclusion. It is difficult. For, many who see you as *difficult* will avoid giving the feedback, precisely because you can be difficult and they do not want to be at the receiving end of your tirade. And, those who dare to give the feedback could be silenced, asked to shut up or just brushed aside. I do realize all these difficulties. As I have stated before, the ego is the biggest barrier.

20

Fear of death is one of the most repressed fears in humans.

DEATH

I have had an interesting association with death. The basic human condition was first disclosed to me in the form of an all pervading, overwhelming fear of my inevitable death. Remember, the post-accident road scene I had witnessed in Delhi that I have described right in the beginning of this book? That incident completely rattled me. It was as if I seriously felt for the first time in my life that I have to die one day. I probed myself closely to understand what was bothering me so severely.

To be precise, it was a fear of facing the situation that I will cease to exist one day.

It was my fear of inevitable non-existence.

Where would my consciousness go?

The physical world will continue the same way, my belongings would continue to exist, life would move on, but where would I be?

I was in panic. I was aghast to see all other persons, going about their lives unconcerned, even though they knew fully well that they were going to die one day. Rationally speaking, the inevitability of death was a reality. Yet why did they not fear death as acutely as I did?

That death is a final curtains-fall was also very true.

The only negligible comfort that I could draw was that, most probably, I was not going to die any time soon. But that did not help either. Because, my next question was: what about people past their middle age? What about elderly people? Do they seem to be so badly shaken? Is it that humankind has learned and practiced to keep these disturbing but real thoughts at bay? I had also, until I had seen this fatal accident, successfully evaded this fundamental question of death. Why couldn't I *go back* to my earlier state where death, despite being a reality, did not bother me to this extent? Soon this fear of death gave way to more fundamental and unanswered questions within me about the meaning of life, aimlessness, search for ultimate fulfillment, and then on to depression, anxiety and emptiness.

Having come thus far in this book, you will realize that human beings keep FUNDAMENTAL UNHAPPINESS nicely under wraps. At worst, it occasionally nudges us or sends a hint. It often exists under our skin, but we distract ourselves, get busy, engage with success, get attached to many *things* in life, blame others, complain and successfully escape the pain within. Fear of death is only one manifestation of this dreaded human condition. Other manifestations are meaninglessness, sense of void, emptiness, anxiety, and depression without any real reason. The problem is that once this inner condition gets revealed, it can never be kept covered under wraps again. James Park has aptly illustrated the irreversibility of the disclosed human condition:

"Once our anxiety has begun to leak out of its interior vault and has left its indelible stain on our everyday life, we might never successfully seal it inside again. The common, ordinary world no longer supplies sufficient orientation. The 'real' world has melted away, becoming a dim background."

Sensitive and perceptive human beings often find themselves in this situation. They might try hard like other *normal* beings to distract, or get busy, but with limited results. They can never get back to their earlier days of successful evasion. It is a painful place to remain stuck in. The best way to handle the situation is to fully acknowledge the condition without treating it as a disease and to stop running away from it. Just the stance of observing it as a passive onlooker substantially reduces the severity of the distress. That is just the beginning. You can step into a life of richness, authenticity and depth. You are more aware than the *others*. You can embark on a journey towards FUNDAMENTAL HAPPINESS. You will progressively find the journey itself joyful. As I have stated before, many illustrious persons have given their creative best from this position of authenticity, in the form of art, writings or movies. And, that gnawing fear of impending death does not bother you anymore.

Coming back to death – researchers have stated that fear of death is one of the most repressed fears in humans.

Existential writers have extensively dealt with this very fundamental fear embedded deep within. It seems the human brain is trained to treat death very pragmatically or intellectually reject it as something that is going to happen eventually and is a fact of life. This very objective and rational approach to death also helps to keep the *irrational* fear of death locked out. Much of mankind is able to do so successfully and, as a result, any idea of fear of death is seen as *irrational*. On the other hand, for all those people to whom the inner condition stands disclosed, fear of death appears to be very real and truthful. For them it is strange that others do not feel the same way. And, no amount of rationalizing, logic or any scientific approach helps to mitigate this dreadful fear.

> **RESEARCHERS HAVE STATED THAT FEAR OF DEATH IS ONE OF THE MOST REPRESSED FEARS IN HUMANS.**

I am not suggesting that you all start scratching yourselves now to discover the fear of death within. That is not necessary. All you need to do is to focus inwards and notice whatever unease you find in your being. Recognize it, observe it and move on. It could be the biggest gift in life. It is not necessary to have felt all the manifestations of our FUNDAMENTAL UNHAPPINESS. Fear of death is just one of them. Amongst the long list of ways in which you suffer the inner unease, existential writers have mentioned *guilt* as one of the manifestations. I can state that I have never been able to recognize existential guilt in me. Whenever I suffered any guilt, I have ascribed it to the wrong things that I might have done. I was never able to discern that uncaused guilt which could be part of our FUNDAMENTAL UNHAPPINESS. I do not dismiss *guilt* as a possible manifestation. It is just that I could not recognize it and this lack of understanding has not been an obstacle in my journey towards FUNDAMENTAL HAPPINESS. *Absurdity* is another manifestation of our basic condition. For those who are interested, *Waiting for Godot* by Samuel Beckett, referred to by me earlier in the section titled, Fundamental Unhappiness is a famous absurdist play where this has been elaborated. Those of you who have felt some of these aspects of deeper existence would have noticed that the dividing line between the different ways we feel this suffering is very thin. They actually merge. It is very difficult to specify where absurdity gives way to void or to meaninglessness. It is not necessary, either. The sum total of the human FUNDAMENTAL UNHAPPINESS and how we avoid it needs to be acknowledged. That is the crucial part.

Allow me to illustrate this with my own struggle with the fear of death. This fear gave way to other issues in me like meaninglessness, emptiness and depression. The lack of fulfillment and enthusiasm was so glaring that depression and melancholy became the general tone of my life. I was diagnosed as suffering from depression. I told myself, with some conviction, that my main problem was depression – due to changed brain chemistry? – And that all other questions about life were only a symptom of this *disease*. I, therefore, did not feel the need to hunt for answers to those questions. That is how I managed a normal life externally. I was doing well in my work life. I think I was also leading a *normal* family life. However, my wife and daughters sometimes sensed a general lack of interest in my daily dealings and at times, pointed it out to me. The moot point is that work and family were some distraction even for a person like me with the inner condition fully disclosed. Other than close family members, no one knew or sensed anything about my suffering.

However, the fear of death was firmly present. It came out in difficult circumstances. I remember having lost a close friend in a road accident. (Somehow, road accidents have been an integral part of my life. I actually met with one myself – I fell asleep while driving!). Visiting the hospital, when my friend was in a critical condition just before his death, was a nightmare. The repressed fear of death had sprung back with such enormity that it crippled me. I skipped his funeral. Attending any funeral often was a challenge for me.

Years later when I was about to lose my father to a brief illness, I could not bear the sight or thought of his death. Once it was clear that he would not survive, I wished that the end would come soon so that I could be past all this quickly! It was unbearable. My fear of death had a paralyzing effect on me. It took me weeks to overcome the trauma.

Finally, I was lucky to have stumbled upon the right kind of literature and thought through the internet, leading to interesting books and a lot of spiritual ideas. This set me on a journey, starting with acknowledgement, without running away. I realized that the more one runs away from the pain, one ends up running away from one's own self. Rather, you need to come closer to yourself, actually connect with your *Self*. The pain may increase, for some time. But that is the only path. My acute suffering was the biggest motivation for adopting the posture of surrender. I had tried everything else. I was on my journey towards FUNDAMENTAL HAPPINESS. Just as you suffer uncaused depression or anxiety, I experienced bouts of uncaused joy on several occasions when I was closer to FUNDAMENTAL HAPPINESS.

During this stage of my life, I lost my mother to cancer. Unlike the way I experienced my father's demise, I was with my mother till her end. I could feel her going away. The fear of death did not bother me, and my response to a very dear person heading towards death was now very different. There was no urge to somehow *fast-forward* the situation. Yes, I was concerned that my mother's suffering should not prolong – but that was from her standpoint. I was keen that the doctor gave her as good a life as possible, as long as she lived. The doctor did do a wonderful job. I was connected to her till the end.

It is said that a spiritually advanced person is connected with the universe. He does not see himself as separate. He is part of the whole. Ken Wilber calls this stage *"transpersonal"*. Eastern philosophies call it *'advaita'* or non-duality. There is a lot of complicated and exhaustive literature on this concept of *'advaita'*, the original source being the *Vedantas*. The limited point I want to make, without getting lost in complex theories, is that at the level of FUNDAMENTAL HAPPINESS, or at a level even close to it, you can feel this oneness with all existence. I felt this wondrous oneness with my mother when she was going. We were like the same being. This was different from when my father went, although I was very close to him too.

We might be very effective in avoiding the deep fear of death, but the fact that death remains a mystery for mankind cannot be denied. There are many very popular, touching stories and films, which have closely dealt with death. In the 70s, hugely popular Hindi movies like *Safar, Anand* or *Achanak* had death as their central theme. Today, society is noisier, with far more distractions and aids for diversions. I doubt whether such themes will work today. Still, no mystery novel or movie is complete without a murder. In some ways, death and the fear of the unknown do tickle us. My guess is that even though the fear of death stays firmly under wraps, it does tickle us without derailing us. Good movies, stories surrounding the theme of death stir us up. We are probably awakened a bit by the deep seated fear, though it remains locked inside. Horror or disaster movies also probably work on this fear of death though the fear does not get fully exposed amongst the audience. Remember the famous movie, *Psycho*?

21

WHY ANOTHER BOOK?

There are a number of books in the market showing you the path towards enlightenment. I have read many of them, and yes, many of them are good books. Once you start understanding the spiritual language, you will easily grasp the essence of all of them. In fact, Eckhart Tolle's *The Power of Now* went on to become a best seller. The language may differ but they all eventually show you the possibility of peace, joy and living in the realm of non-duality, or 'adviata', as we understand in Indian terminology.

So, where was the need for yet another book?

I was a little unhappy with many books in the market on spirituality, which start with high sounding concepts like, *"Awaken your spirit"* without explaining what it is all about. There is no short cut to spiritual growth. There is a lot to internalize and everything has to be put in perspective. It is serious business but not rocket science either. Things are pretty straightforward. Yet I did not want to trivialize the matter. I have not used any complex research or theory either. Mostly I have tried to relate to everyday life. I wanted the starting point to be to question the degree of pain we carry, often unknowingly.

My urge was, to first and foremost, reach out to most people leading wretched lives of depression and despair. I wanted them to benefit from the story of my own struggle with depression and meaninglessness, before attaining relief. Unfortunately all that suffering is categorized as mental illness and doctors start treating them accordingly. I wished to underline that many cases that manifested in depression, anxiety, meaninglessness and despair, can have no cause at all and are not cases of mental illness. More importantly, by treating such people as medically ill, we are, perhaps, pulling them down to become *normal* individuals, whereas, the way out is further movement upwards to a higher level of consciousness. I had this strong urge to demonstrate that the perceived mental illness is actually a sign of growth, which should not be blocked through medication. While doing so, I felt the motivation to articulate how I have myself suffered the same way for years before hitting the right path. And, choosing that path is neither difficult, nor some make-believe fairy tale prospect. I am not talking about complicated mental illness here. Diseases like schizophrenia, bipolar disorder, OCD may have their own dimensions and I am the last person to start an argument with the psychiatric community on those ailments. It is true, however, that there are philosophers who have even questioned the divide between the sane and the insane. Michel Foucault may be good example of being one such.

My focus is purely on the existential kind of depression – uncaused. People who suffer depression or anguish need not be insane, yet they may have lost all taste for life. My focus is to underline that such form of despair, meaninglessness, or emptiness is not a mental illness. It is actually an opportunity to make that paradigm shift in life and move to something you could not imagine. I was ready to give a peek into my life for the readers to see for themselves what is possible. This journey towards bliss is available to all humans.

Unfortunately, the vast majority of *normal* beings may not have the strong motivation to make that internal shift. They will probably say that they are fine even as they could, at some stage in their lives, suddenly be confronted with some basic, hard questions about life, for which no ready answers are available. They might find this book useful, if these thoughts remain at the back of their minds. The plethora of books in this area is an indication of how much more fundamental existence is currently being questioned. You would have also noticed that in the present age more and more people externally demonstrate impatience, aggression, intemperance, collectively all of which could be classified as the human angst. Going by Ken Wilber's theory, and also largely written by Eckhart Tolle in *A New Earth*, it could be an indication of the evolutionary journey of human consciousness. Mankind may have to go through a lot of collective pain before the species transcends into a peaceful life. But Tolle has given only a passing reference to his own suffering at the beginning of *The Power of Now*. Wilber has been largely theoretical and research based. I felt there was a need to build, with the help of simple language and practical examples from our lives, on the opportunity of using our suffering to go beyond.

> **I WAS READY TO GIVE A PEEK INTO MY LIFE FOR THE READERS TO SEE FOR THEMSELVES WHAT IS POSSIBLE. THIS JOURNEY TOWARDS BLISS IS AVAILABLE TO ALL HUMANS.**

James Park too has described the human suffering in great detail, and shared experiences from his own life. He has also shown the way of possibly going beyond. Unfortunately, with his existential background, his book, *Our Existential Predicament* remains a grim description of the situation. If I have understood him correctly, his prospect of living a level below FUNDAMENTAL HAPPINESS, that he calls authentic existence, displays the characteristic grimness and seriousness that go with existentialist writings. I have all respect for existential thoughts. They are almost an essential resting place before you move on. Park has also accurately captured the need and possibility of going beyond our basic condition with all the accompanying pitfalls and struggles. But this depiction of authentic existence is grim to the core. Only at one place, while referring to Martin Heidegger, Park brings out that this state of being can also be joyful. There is practically no possibility, according to Park, of leading a so-called *normal* life while being close to FUNDAMENTAL HAPPINESS. The only meaningful pursuit you could carry on with either at the level of authentic existence, or as an existentially free person, according to Park, is to help others traverse the same path. I do believe that once a person tastes awareness, there emerges a strong urge to spread this awareness, which is why I wrote this book. I also wanted to share that life one step below FUNDAMENTAL HAPPINESS is joyful, insightful, deep, and, indeed, you can pursue almost any goal in life, as long as it does not come from your ego. I also thought it necessary to hold out the clear prospect of leading practical daily lives, have some ambitions and a mission with complete awareness of what these are about and lead a joyful life of fulfillment. In the end, no matter what nomenclature we use – spirituality, enlightenment, wisdom – it is all about awareness. As a spiritual person, you are more aware than the *normal*. You are also more conscious. That's all. Yet this one step brings so much fundamental difference to our lives. At first reading, it might look difficult. Believe me; the difficulty arises only because our minds are trained to shirk pain, suffering, and the ugly. That is how we learn the trick of denial, and lead entire lives of unawareness or unconsciousness.

Truly speaking, much of humanity is living like patients suffering from severe pain placed under deep anesthesia. The patient does not feel his pain, but is it a life worth living? Would it not be better if the patient could rid himself of the pain and did not need the heavy dose of anesthesia?

I have tried to keep my book from being content heavy. Much like religious texts, many books on spirituality get complicated, theoretical and heavy at the cost of losing the moot point. I have tried to keep it very simple. After a few rounds of reading you might realize that matters of spirituality are pretty straightforward.

I have a strong urge to suggest that this aspect of practical living should be introduced in school curriculums. Children have less resistance in themselves. The aged too, often give up on life and their level of resistance decreases. The highest degree of resistance will be found from the teenager to the middle aged, especially the very successful ones. I must concede, though, that there are many examples of highly successful people who have come closer to the spirit. They have been able to balance their practical and spiritual lives. Many of them have gone a step further and made it their life's mission to improve the condition of the not-so-fortunate people. They display a strong urge to give back something to society. Hopefully in times to come we will find more such people in the world.

22

^AWISH

I began this book with my story. It is about where I was and where I found myself years later. When I was first exposed to my depression, anxiety, meaninglessness and void, I felt that I had become completely different from others. They were *normal*. I was not. All attempts to come back to the *normal* existence failed miserably thereafter. I had changed. Forever.

While suffering, I had fantasized the possibility of finding a simple exit from this state and going back to my supposedly joyful existence. I had even indulged in wishful thinking: that this suffering was just an illusion, a horrible dream, and if only I could shake myself off this dream, life would be back to normal again.

What happened subsequently was not much different from this fantasy. I was just a few steps away from FUNDAMENTAL HAPPINESS. Depression and joy looked like two sides of the same coin. It is like a revolving door – you can move into and out of suffering, and into and out of FUNDAMENTAL HAPPINESS. Once you stay close to FUNDAMENTAL HAPPINESS by adopting some major shifts in your lives, you can live life close to FUNDAMENTAL HAPPINESS. Your awareness acts as a solid foundation that will not allow you to fall all the way down to the suffering pit.

Am I suggesting that you lead a life of abstinence? The answer is:

No. Take a pause and enjoy your life like before from a different vantage point.

You would have encountered people who, by their very nature, do not crave or ask for much. They seem to be peaceful. They naturally have very little resistance in them. They are not likely to be the first ones to get rattled if the flight gets delayed. Does that mean that if you are the opposite kind – the tense, restless kind, or in a rush, then you are not better off? Rather than questioning yourself this way, I would suggest you first focus on allowing yourself to try out most things in life, which you think will give you a sense of happiness or satisfaction or purpose. Then question yourself honestly. Build awareness. Awareness lends you the probability of adopting the posture of surrender to move closer to FUNDAMENTAL HAPPINESS. The big difference is that the person who does not crave much and is naturally peaceful may not have the benefit of awareness. His persona is that of acceptance. So he is likely to be more peaceful. But attaining peace through awareness gives you a richer life. It makes you a wiser person. And this awareness will be a solid platform for the rest of your life, always holding you above that threshold of almost-FUNDAMENTAL HAPPINESS. This is real and durable, and not like the security blankets we adopt to hide ourselves from the underlying FUNDAMENTAL UNHAPPINESS.

Today, I find myself joyfully different from the *normal* and when I look around I recognize other *not-so-normal* beings who are on the brink of a journey that they are unaware of or unwilling to take. You can notice the basic human condition just under their skin. But try telling them about the way out. They are likely to think you are crazy. I feel bad for them. A book is a better way to reach out. For, then, you are not addressing someone in particular. There is less resistance in a reader as compared to when the same person is lectured. Let us hope this works. Also my guess, and hope, is that the sheer severity and all encompassing nature of this collective human misery will itself be the cause for much of humanity to move towards FUNDAMENTAL HAPPINESS in the years to come. The burden of managing this pain would be just too much for us and, hopefully, we will give up. Remember, most often the pangs of uncaused depression, despair or anxiety that we suffer are messages from our inner being, nudging us to allow ourselves to grow.

Good luck!

On the brink of a JOURNEY...

You may contact the author on the platforms mentioned below:

email : chatterjee.deepak33@gmail.com

Face book : www.facebook.com/deepak.chatterjee.944

Twitter : www.twitter.com/Deepak33c

Blog: http://fundamentalhappiness.blogspot.com